"Are You Te... A Computer Program To Find The Perfect Woman?"

"Yes."

"So how did you end up with me, Justice? There's no way I could have been on your short list."

"You weren't. It would seem the computer program contained a flaw. I didn't want them. I wanted you."

At the first touch of her soft form colliding against his hard angles, he discovered he'd made a serious miscalculation. Whatever they'd experienced all those months ago hadn't dissipated over time as he'd anticipated. If anything the craving had grown progressively worse. It might not be logical, but it was unquestionably true.

He lowered his head toward hers. "And I'll do anything—and I do mean anything—to have you."

* * *

Dear Reader,

When I was little, I dreamed of my "perfect" man. He'd be tall (six feet two inches, to be exact). He'd have wavy black hair and blue eyes (sinfully handsome, naturally). He'd be rich (of course). And we'd have ten children (oh, yes, I was truly insane). My mother asked me who would feed us since I couldn't cook and would get so lost in a book that I'd forget to feed myself, let alone all these children.

The man I ultimately married missed the mark by two inches, but hey, who's counting? His hair is the color of sand. He does have those blue eyes. And to me, he'll always be sinfully handsome because my eyes see all that makes him such an incredible person. Instead of ten children, we have one—beloved by us both and if not perfect, darn close.

I learned over the years that there is no such thing as the "perfect" man, any more than the "perfect" woman. The trick is to find the person perfect for you. And I think my husband and I came very, very close.

Which brings me to my current story about a brilliant scientist who creates a program to find the perfect wife. What he ends up with is far, far different (of course). But maybe, just maybe, she'll show him that what they create together is perfect for them. I hope you enjoy *Nothing Short of Perfect* and I wish for you the "perfect" mate!

Warmly,

Day Leclaire

DAY
LECLAIRE

NOTHING SHORT
OF PERFECT

Recycling programs
for this product may
not exist in your area.

ISBN-13: 978-0-373-73134-3

NOTHING SHORT OF PERFECT

Copyright © 2011 by Day Totton Smith

DAY LECLAIRE

USA TODAY bestselling author Day Leclaire is described by Harlequin Books as "one of our most popular writers ever!" Day's tremendous worldwide popularity has made her a member of Harlequin's "Five Star Club," with sales of well over five million books. She is a three-time winner of both a Colorado Award of Excellence and a Golden Quill Award. She's won RT Book Reviews Career Achievement and Love and Laughter Awards, a Holt Medallion and a Booksellers' Best Award. She has also received an impressive ten nominations for the prestigious Romance Writers of America's RITA® Award.

Day's romances touch the heart and make you care about her characters as much as she does. In Day's own words, "I adore writing romances, and can't think of a better way to spend each day." For more information, visit Day at her website, www.dayleclaire.com.

To Rita Doerr.
Thank you so much for your assistance with the
Prologue of this book and helping me keep it real.
And to the imperfect people in my life,
who make my life so perfect.
All my love.

Prologue

"Can you hear me, sir? Can you tell us your name?"

Pain exploded all around him. His head. His arm. His chest. Something had happened to him, but he didn't understand what. He sensed movement and heard a siren. What the hell? Was he in an ambulance?

"Sir? What's your name?"

"St. John. Jus— Jus—" The words escaped, sounding slurred and tinny to his ears. For some reason he couldn't coordinate tongue and mouth well enough to give his first name, forcing him to settle for the closest approximation. "Jus St. John. What…?"

The man seemed to understand the simple question. "You were in a car accident, Mr. St. John. I'm a paramedic. We're transporting you to the hospital where they'll treat your injuries."

"Wait," someone else said. A woman this time. Soothing voice. "Did he say St. John? Justice St. John? *The* Justice St. John."

"You know this guy?"

"Heard of him. He's some famous inventor. Robotics. Runs a company called Sinjin. A bit of a recluse. Worth billions."

The man swore. "Which means if he doesn't make it, guess who's going to get blamed? We'd better call this in to the supervisor and alert her we have a VIP. She'll want to get ahead of the media circus."

Someone asked another question. Endless questions. Why the hell wouldn't they leave him alone? "Do you have any allergies, Mr. St. John?" the voice persisted. Then louder, "Any medical conditions we should know about?"

"No. Can't move."

"We have you immobilized as a precaution, Mr. St. John." The soothing voice again. "That's why you can't move."

"BP is dropping. We need to get him stabilized. Mr. St. John, do you remember how the car accident occurred?"

Of course he remembered. An idiot driver was texting or yakking on a cell phone and lost control of the car. God, he hurt. Justice pried open one eye. His world appeared in a blur of color and movement. A harsh light struck him and he flinched from it.

"Stop it, damn you," he growled. Okay, that came out better.

"Pupils reactive. IV's in. Repeat vitals. Let the supervisor know we're gonna need a neurologist, just to be on the safe side. Request Forrest. No point in taking any chances. Mr. St. John, can you hear me?"

Justice swore again. "Shouting. Stop shouting."

"We're taking you to Lost Valley Memorial Hospital. Is there someone we can contact for you?"

Pretorius. His uncle. An image flashed across Justice's mind, of tawny St. John eyes set in a hound dog face and broad shoulders hunched over a computer keyboard. They could call his uncle. They'd need the phone number since it was unlisted and right now Justice couldn't think of it through the roar of pain. He tried to explain the problem and found his tongue refused to twist around the words.

And then Justice realized that even if he could explain, Pretorius wouldn't come. Oh, he'd want to, no question of that. He'd be desperate to. But like the impenetrable wall that prevented Justice from giving his rescuers the necessary phone number, an equally impenetrable wall prevented Pretorius from leaving their estate, his fear too great to overcome.

And that's when it struck him. He had no one. No one who gave a damn on an intimate level whether he lived or died. No one who could take care of his uncle if he didn't survive. No one to carry on his legacy or benefit from what he had to offer. How had it happened? Why had he allowed it to happen? When had he cut himself off so completely?

He'd lived in isolation these past years, keeping himself distant from emotional attachment, from the pain life had a habit of inflicting. And now he'd die alone and unmourned except by those who respected him in a professional capacity. He'd wanted to hold himself apart from the rest of the world, craved the solitude. Wanted desperately to just be left the hell alone. And he'd succeeded. But at what price? He could see it now, see so clearly how year after year, winter after winter, a fresh layer of ice had coated his heart and soul until now he didn't think he'd ever be warm again.

Once upon a time he'd known springtime, had known the warmth of a summer day and the love of a woman. Woman? Hell, she'd been nothing more than a girl. A girl whose name he'd attempted to bury so deep in the recesses of his mind that it would vanish from his memory, and yet who had branded herself on the very fiber of his being. Daisy. She'd been the one who'd proved to him once and for all that emotions were an unnecessary evil. And now what was he? What had he allowed himself to become?

"Mr. St. John? Is there someone we should notify?"

"No." He succumbed to the painful truth, allowing the blackness to carry him away. Allowing the painful memories to slip into some dark, nebulous place.

There was no one.

One

"What's the status of your latest computer run?" Justice asked.

Pretorius grimaced, peering at the screen from behind the same black-rimmed computer glasses he'd owned for the past twenty years. "Based on the parameters you've given me, I've found half a dozen possibilities that score at eighty percent probability or higher."

"Hell, is that all?"

"We're lucky to have found even that many women considering your list of requirements. I mean, no one with black hair? What was with that?"

Justice grimaced. He had no intention of explaining any of his prerequisites, especially that one. "Well, if my choice is limited to six, then I'll just have to make do."

"Make *do?*" Pretorius swiveled his computer chair in a swift one-eighty, eyes the same unique shade of gold as Justice's glittering in outrage. "Are you mad? You're talking about the future Mrs. Sinjin, Incorporated here."

Justice waved that aside. "Next issue. Are they a half dozen you can handle having here at the estate? There's no way you can avoid running into them on occasion. It's not like I can keep them locked up and out of sight. Something tells me they won't agree to that particular condition."

Pretorius shuddered. "Well, so long as it's one at a time and not all of them together in a horde. Can't handle a horde." His chair drifted closer, the casters skating freely across the wooden floor. "Justice, are you sure you want to go through with this?"

"I'm positive."

"It's because of that car wreck, isn't it? It caused more than memory glitches. It's changed you. Changed your long-term goals. Changed how you look at the world."

Justice retreated behind an icy facade, one that never failed to stop even the most pushy person dead in his tracks. Not that it intimidated his uncle. Damn it all. He'd do anything to avoid this conversation, perhaps because it sliced too close to the heart of the matter.

Without a word, he crossed the generous expanse of the computer room and picked up a silver sphere consisting of small interlocking sections, each one engraved with a mathematical symbol. It was one of his inventions, one he hadn't released to the general public. He called it Rumi, short for ruminate, since he played with it whenever he needed to work through a problem—which was basically most of the time.

Maybe he should have called it Obs for obsessive.

Pretorius pushed off with the toe of his sneaker and sent his computer chair shooting back toward his endless bank of computers and monitors. "You can't avoid the discussion, Justice. If you plan to go forward with your plan, I deserve the truth."

"I know." Justice's fingers moved restlessly across Rumi's surface, pushing and pulling the various sections until he'd transformed the sphere into a cylinder. Instead of smooth and flowing, it appeared jagged and disjointed, the symbols a chaotic jumble. These days the shapes were always a chaotic jumble. They'd been that way for over a year, a full six months before the accident.

He changed the topic, hoping it would distract his uncle. "Will all the women be at the symposium for Engineering into the Next Millennium?"

"Ridiculous title," Pretorius muttered.

"Agreed. Stay on target. Will they be there?"

"I made sure of it. Two weren't planning to attend, but I—" He hesitated. "Let's just say I arranged for them to change their mind."

Justice knew better than to request specifics. "Excellent."

"Talk to me, boy. Why? Why are you doing this?"

Justice shook his head, not certain he could put it into words. He attempted to coax the cylinder into a double helix while struggling to give voice to the realization he'd made after his accident. How did he explain the nothingness that had become his life over the past few years? Hell, he couldn't remember the last time he'd felt any emotion, whether anger or happiness or something—*anything*—in between.

With each passing day his feelings, the drive to invent, even his ambition had slowly iced over. While each minute ticked relentlessly by, everything that made him a "normal"— and he used the word in its loosest possible context—living, breathing human eked away. Soon only a cold, hard shell of a man would remain. He tossed Rumi aside, frustrated by its refusal to assume a clean-cut functional shape.

"It's just something I need you to accept," Justice finally said. "For my sake."

"Call and cancel," Pretorius urged. "Before you do something we both regret."

"I can't do that. I'm the keynote speaker."

Pretorius switched gears. "What in the bloody hell are you

supposed to say about engineering into the next millennia? That's a thousand damn years. It's impossible to predict whether there will even be a human race in a thousand years, let alone the status of engineering over that period of time."

"And you claim I swear a lot."

"What can I say? Your vices are rubbing off on me. Justice, you haven't made a public appearance in five years. This isn't the time to change that."

"I haven't made a public appearance in five years because I haven't had a damn thing worth saying for five years. When I do have a damn thing worth saying, I'll start making public appearances again. Until then, I can manage one little symposium without falling flat on my face."

"The media will be all over this one little symposium now that your name is connected with it. After such a lengthy absence they'll expect you to offer something of vital significance. I don't suppose you have something of vital significance to say to them?"

Justice waved that aside. "Don't worry about my speech, old man. I'll make something up. The ironic part is, if I claim it's possible, some fool in the audience will believe me and go out there and invent it. Win, win."

"But why? Just give me one good reason why you're doing this."

Justice dropped a hand to his uncle's shoulder with a sigh. He knew going into this would be hard on Pretorius, but something had to change. Now. Before time overcame opportunity. "I haven't invented anything in a solid year."

"Your creativity is just blocked. We can find a way to unblock it without going to such extremes."

"I don't see how it's possible for my creativity to be blocked since I don't possess any. I'm an engineer."

This time Pretorius sighed. "Inventors are creative people, Justice."

"That's a damn lie and you know it. Now take it back."

It was a running joke between them, but for some reason it lacked its usual humor. Maybe because he found it more and more difficult to laugh about his current situation.

"I understand that you need a woman. I don't object to that. Go...go find someone." To Justice's amusement the tips of Pretorius's ears turned bright red. "Let nature take its course. Once it has, you can come back all refreshed and revitalized."

"It's not that simple. I need—"

How did he explain? Ever since the accident he realized he needed more than just some temporary woman. More than a single night, or even a month of single nights. He longed for something permanent. Something enduring. Something that he could count on today and tomorrow and next month and next year. Someone who gave a damn. Someone he could call when...if—

"Mr. St. John? Is there someone we should notify?" Those words continued to haunt him, even after all these months. As did his answer, *"No." There was no one.*

"I need more," Justice whispered.

His uncle fell silent, then nodded, reading between the lines. He understood the subtext, even if he was reluctant to accept it. "It means you'll have to stop swearing so much. Granted, it would make for a nice change."

Justice's mouth twitched. "I'll work on that," he assured gravely.

"It would also mean we'd have some decent food around here." Pretorius warmed to the idea. "And a clean house."

"Somehow I don't think the woman I marry would appreciate knowing I picked her because I needed a housekeeper with privileges." Justice leaned over his uncle's shoulder and pushed a button. The laser printer sprang to life, shooting out sheet after sheet of material. "Which brings me back to my main concern. If I marry, you'll have to put up with her, too. You've read the information on these women. Can you handle one of them living here permanently?"

Pretorius frowned. "Is that why you haven't married before this? Were you worried about how I'd react to having our home invaded?"

Invaded. Justice suppressed a sigh. This was going to be a tough sell. "No, I haven't married because I've never found someone I could tolerate for longer than a week."

His uncle nodded morosely. "That's where my computer program comes in, I assume? I've done my best to transform the Pretorius Program from a business application to a more personal one. The parameters remain similar. Finding the perfect wife isn't all that different from finding the perfect employee."

"Exactly. It just requires inputting different data." He ran through his requirements. "An engineer, therefore rational and in control of her emotions. Brilliant, of course. I can't handle foolish women. Physically attractive would be a bonus. But she must be logical. Kind. Someone who won't make waves. And she must be able to handle isolation."

"I thought we were talking about a woman."

"If she's an engineer, chances are she'll already possess most of those qualities. More important, she'll fit in around here."

"Okay, fine." Pretorius straightened, assuming a professional attitude. "If you're determined to go through with this, I've narrowed the choices down to a half-dozen women, all of whom will be attending the symposium."

"With a little help from you."

"That was the easy part," Pretorius said grimly.

He picked up the stack of papers the printer had coughed out and fanned through them. Justice caught a glimpse of charts and graphs, photos, as well as curricula vitae, and— dear God—what appeared to be reports from a private investigator. Never let it be said his uncle wasn't thorough.

"And the hard part?"

"Women are odd creatures, Justice. They tend to have a

negative reaction when you invite them for a cup of coffee in one breath and in the next tell them you want a wife."

"Well, hell." He hadn't thought about that.

"You could always make up an excuse for needing a bride so quickly. I'm sure they'll buy it. After all, you are The Great Justice St. John. Or so all the scientific journals claim."

"Oh, for—"

"Or you can listen to the not-quite-as-great Pretorius St. John, who's actually considered that small detail."

"And?"

"And you're not attending the symposium in order to find a wife. You're there to find an apprentice."

His uncle caught him off guard with an abrupt left onto an unmarked road. It took Justice a moment to brake, make a swift U-turn and input the new course. "I don't need an apprentice."

"Yes, you do. At least, that's what you're going to tell these women. It's the only way to get them in your clutches. Once you settle on someone you think you can stand for longer than a month, get her to move out here. Work with her for a bit. Get her to fall in love with you and then marry her. That way she won't think you're some sort of kook. Or with luck, once she realizes you are, it'll be too late. She'll be wedded and bedded, with possibly a TGJSJ, Jr. on the way. And maybe she'll even cook and clean just because that's what women do." Pretorius shoved the stack of papers into Justice's hands. "In the meantime, study these. The symposium lasts three days which divides out to two candidates a day. You have that long to come back with an apprentice/wife we both can live with."

"And if it doesn't work out?"

His uncle folded his arms across his chest. "I've been thinking about this. And even though I don't want a strange woman wandering around here, poking her nose in where it doesn't belong, I've realized something."

"Which is?" Justice asked warily.

Pretorius stabbed a stubby finger in his direction. "You have a lot of knowledge and ability going to waste. You have an obligation to share it with others. Even if she doesn't work out as a wife, you'll have invested in the future either by providing inspiration for some brilliant young thing or, if you get lucky, you'll pass on your genetic code to another generation."

"That's a hell of a way to put it."

"Don't forget this was your idea, boy. Whether you realize it or not, that genius label you carry around comes with a price tag attached. You owe a debt to the universe."

"I gather the universe sent a bill?" Justice asked dryly.

"And you neglected to pay. That's why you're blocked. You've hoarded your knowledge instead of spreading it around. If the wife thing doesn't work out at least you'll have passed along your know-how to a worthy successor. And *that* I can live with since it'll only be temporary."

"And if she happens to fall in love and it's not temporary?"

Pretorius narrowed his eyes. "You think she's the only one who'll fall in love? Not the both of you?"

Justice knew better than to expect that. He doubted he was capable of love any longer. "Just her," he confirmed.

"In that case, I like my dinner served at six."

Justice St. John.

Daisy Marcellus stopped dead in her tracks the instant she caught sight of the familiar name centered on the Coronation Hotel's advertisement placard. Late-afternoon sunlight cascaded across the stunning black-and-white photo of him, threatening to bring her to her knees. Her bright fuchsia carryall slipped from her grasp and tumbled to the floor, pens and stickers and trinkets for toddlers spilling at her feet.

It was him.

Granted, a much different him than the one she'd known

a full decade ago. This man appeared harder, far fiercer than the version she'd known. Oh, his eyes were the same, betraying that heartbreaking wariness she remembered so vividly, like an animal constantly on the alert for danger. But that wariness seemed more intense now, and shaded with cynicism.

She studied each line of the revealing photograph, searching for other changes and finding them all too easily. Time had weathered creases into strong masculine features, the deepest ones bracketing a mouth set in far too severe a line. He'd acquired a grim edge over the years, a hardness that she could only hope was at the instigation of the photographer for overall effect, rather than a true reflection of the man.

Despite the worrisome changes, desire vied with a bottomless longing, while desperate joy cascaded through her. She reached out to trace his image, a shaky smile slipping across her face. After all these years, they'd found each other again. Well, okay. So they hadn't found each other. *She* had found *him*. But what did that matter?

Would he be equally delighted to see her? Would he even remember her? Considering how much she'd changed, possibly not. But she remembered him, and she also remembered every incredible summery moment of those short three months they'd spent together. She laughed out loud, drawing attention to herself. Not that she cared. Not when today meant she'd get to see Justice again.

Daisy stooped and shoved her belongings back into her carryall while she read the information on the placard. It would seem Justice had made a name for himself in the engineering world. Well, good for him. Even better, in just five short minutes his keynote speech would start. Excellent. She had nothing else scheduled for this late in the afternoon. Surely no one would object if she crashed the party, considering she and Justice were old friends—not to mention old lovers.

In fact, he'd been her first lover, the most special of them all, and she'd never forgotten him. Never known a love as wonderful or carefree as what she'd shared with him. Never found a man who quite equaled him. Generous. Patient. Kind. Someone who embraced life despite the turmoil of his past. Oh, she couldn't wait to see him again!

A pair of men stood outside the conference room, checking the badges the attendees all wore before allowing them entry. She waited until they were distracted to slip past and into the jam-packed room. People already lined the back wall, having given up on finding a vacant seat. Others milled in the aisles. Finally, she spotted an empty spot near the front row. She didn't really want to sit that close to the stage, but she'd feel even more uncomfortable standing in the back with the masses of engineers when she considered herself as far from being one of them as a butterfly was from a calculator.

For one thing, she'd dressed for a book signing, not a conference. Most of the attendees wore suits and ties, though she considered it a more casual, absentminded professor version than strict Wall Street "businessman" attire. Her breezy slacks and blousy red shirt—perfect for autographing children's storybooks—might as well have come with a sign that said: Alien being here. Give her the hairy eyeball until she makes a break for it.

For another, she hadn't understood a single word anyone had spoken since she walked into the place. She'd overheard any number of conversations, but she didn't understand Basic Geek, even though once upon a time Justice had attempted to teach her.

And finally, with the exception of a few women, the place reeked of testosterone. Not that she had anything against testosterone, but the sheer overwhelming number of men made her feel like a plump pigeon dropped among a roomful of cats.

Slipping into the vacant seat, she smiled at the men on

either side of her. They didn't smile back. Instead they seemed
to dissect her with their gaze, and not in a sexual way. It was
almost as though she represented an equation they couldn't
solve. And maybe she did.

Right when she was on the verge of bolting, the lights
dimmed and a portly man approached the podium. Whispered
comments filtered through the room while everyone settled
into their seats. The man didn't waste any time, but got right
to his introduction of Justice St. John. He ran through an
impressive list of credentials and accomplishments, told
a brief, dry story that, based on the chuckles peppering
the auditorium, was meant to be funny. Maybe it was an
engineering thing, but she didn't get it. Finished, he stepped
aside and glanced expectantly toward the left side of the stage.

Silence drenched the auditorium and people strained
forward, watching eagerly for the keynote speaker. And then
he appeared, sweeping across the stage with a feline grace
that she remembered from their youth. Memories crashed
over her. That day he'd stepped into her parents' home, a
feral panther waiting to attack or be attacked. The lines he'd
drawn to keep himself neatly boxed in and everyone else
boxed out. "Respect the line," he'd ordered. A line she'd taken
such delight in pushing. Erasing. Redrawing. The amazing
night at the lake where their clothes had slipped away and
their bodies had melded with such perfection. That blissful
innocence that had tumbled into passionate knowledge.

Justice's gaze brushed the audience with impatient disdain
and then he launched into incomprehensible Engineering
Geek, which was clearly several levels up from Basic Geek.
Despite understanding only one word in twenty, the deep,
rough tones of his voice held her as mesmerized as everyone
else in the audience.

He'd changed in the years since they'd last been together,
changed beyond belief. But then, so had she. Would she have
recognized him if they'd passed on the street? She frowned.

Possibly. If she looked hard she could just make out the boy overwhelmed by the man he'd become.

"Why didn't I think of that?" the man beside her muttered. A whisper of consensus swept around him.

"Think of what?" Daisy asked.

The man turned to look at her, outrage flashing behind thick glasses. "His suggestions for future inventions. Weren't you listening?"

"Not really," she admitted. "I was too preoccupied looking." A few snickers greeted her comment.

"I swear, when it comes to creating robotic sensors and actuators St. John is the best on the planet," an awestruck whisper came from the row in front of her.

"Especially robotics in relationship to autonomous cooperation with humans," an answering mutter drifted from behind, one equally awestruck.

Interesting. She returned her attention to Justice...and her self-appointed task of looking. She hadn't a clue what all that meant, but color her impressed if he was considered the best on the entire planet. But at what cost? She studied him more carefully.

His features were harder and more defined than they'd been at eighteen. Okay, nearly eighteen. Seriously, what difference did a few weeks make? His eyes were still that dangerous blaze of tawny gold, just like a jungle cat. His hair stopped a shade shy of ebony, the texture rich and dark. He wore it nearly as long now as he did all those years ago, as though far more weighty matters occupied his mind than something so insignificant as getting a haircut. He'd disdained wearing a suit and settled instead on a black shirt and slacks which seemed to swallow all the light on the stage leaving him shrouded in shadows.

He was Hades escaped from the Underworld and everything feminine within her shivered in response to the threat he posed.

Where had the Justice she remembered gone and who was this creature who'd taken his place? He'd changed in some ineffable way that defied her ability to identify. He'd always possessed a logical nature, governed by exquisite self-control. Before, that control hadn't been so reserved or icy. There'd been an openness to him that had allowed her to break through his barriers and lose herself in all that made him the remarkable person he'd been. Laughter had come easily to him, delight in their world a natural part of his personality, his attitude as brilliant as the spill of hot, golden sunshine that had encased them that long-ago summer.

Looking at him now, she realized that had all changed. He wasn't open, but locked up tight. She suspected he rarely laughed. And far from being delighted with the world, he regarded it with a cynical edge that eclipsed that hot, golden sunshine, leaving behind a cold, impenetrable darkness.

What had happened to him? It crushed her to see that he didn't resemble the character she'd created for her storybooks, the one based on her memories of him. How could she have gotten it so wrong? When she'd imagined what sort of metamorphosis he'd undergo transitioning from youth to adult, she'd never, ever conceived *this*.

Just then his gaze settled on her and something odd passed between them. Did he recognize her? Did he remember, even after all this time? Not likely, since her appearance had changed so dramatically in the past decade. His eyes gleamed beneath the overhead lights, like tarnished gold, yet lit with the fire of want.

And that's when Daisy decided. No matter what, before she left here she'd find out what had happened to Justice. She'd take the opportunity, once and for all, to deal with that long-ago past, one she'd never been able to forget. One that she'd used as a measuring stick in every relationship she'd had since their time together. She'd prove to herself that what they'd experienced wasn't so special since, clearly, he was no longer that amazing person he'd once been.

And then, finally, she'd be able to put him back in the box from which she'd released him…and move on.

He didn't want to be here. Didn't want to deliver a speech he not only didn't believe in, but one that involved shoveling the most bull he'd ever attempted in his twenty-eight years. He'd been in Miami Beach for less than a day and already he'd reached the conclusion that it was an abysmal waste of his time.

The minute he arrived, he'd checked into his suite, unpacked his bag and then went after the first name on his list. Why waste time, right? Dorothy Salyer stood just a few inches shy of his own six-foot-three-inch frame and seemed quietly attractive. There was no questioning her intelligence. Knowing the requirements Pretorius had incorporated into his program, all the women would be brilliant. But Dorothy— or Dot, as she'd insisted he call her (shudder)—had been even more shy than his uncle and utterly incapable of stringing even a half-dozen words together.

Strike one.

The second woman on the list was neither tall nor attractive and she never shut up, at least not once she found herself in the presence of The. Great. Justice. St. *John!* She even put the little italic on the John every single frigging time she said his name, which was so often he was tempted to change it then and there. He didn't know if she hoped to impress with her unending staccato chatter, but she'd definitely succeeded in terrorizing. He barely made it through coffee.

Strike two.

Deciding not to waste any further time, he went after the third woman. She proved to be quite delightful (a pleasant change). Pretty (a plus). Normal (a big plus). Intelligent (of course). He almost offered her the position of apprentice then and there. He probably would have if she hadn't chosen that moment to mention that she considered herself a city girl at heart, adored the cultural opportunities Chicago provided and couldn't imagine living anywhere other than the Windy City and—worst of all—she survived on takeout since she couldn't cook.

Third strike and he was almost ready to call it quits. Or he would have if not for a few salient points.

A. He liked women.

B. He liked sitting and having a quiet, adult conversation with a woman.

C. His uncle, damn him to hell and back, was right. He'd hoarded his knowledge instead of spreading it around. Worse, the level of isolation to which he'd dedicated himself had caused a certain stagnation in his intellectual processes, thus his inability to work.

D. The computer program wasn't working.

And that damnable E. Nothing had changed since his accident. He still needed…more. Wanted to take a passing shot at normalcy. To have a life. To feel again, even if he wasn't capable of the sort of depths of emotion romantics ascribed to. To have a family. Children. A legacy.

Which brought him to the woman in the red blouse. For some reason, he couldn't take his eyes off her. She struck some odd note that resonated deep within him, something that tickled a memory, though he couldn't quite place it. All he knew for certain was that he wanted her with a gut-wrenching desire he hadn't experienced in ages. Maybe ever. Which begged a single, urgent question.

Why the hell wasn't she on the list of candidates?

There must be something wrong with her, something the computer defined as unacceptable. Not her looks. Coltishly slender and fine-boned, she epitomized the type of woman he found most appealing. Even better, she was a blonde, the ruler-straight length streaked with just about every permutation of that color. Her features fell somewhere between elegant and fey, except for her mouth, which he could only describe as sultry. So, if it wasn't her appearance, why had she been eliminated from consideration?

Not smart enough? She couldn't be lacking in intelligence, not considering her presence at the symposium. Possibly he had set the intellectual standard a shade on the high side. Perhaps he could lower the bar an IQ point or two if she fell outside the parameters he'd predetermined. He ran through the list he'd given Pretorius again. Physically attractive. Big red check. An engineer. She was here, wasn't she? Double check. That left logical, kind and someone who could handle isolation and wouldn't make waves.

Maybe the computer had deduced in its inimitable fashion that she wasn't logical. Well, hell. He'd be willing to settle for reasonable if she didn't quite qualify as full-blooded rational. Kind? She looked kind to him. So, let's make that a check with a question mark. Perhaps the isolation had caused her to be rejected. He mentally flagged that for future reference. If they put their minds to it, they could find a way around that particular problem. Which left someone who didn't make waves… A nonissue, really. He was a man, wasn't he? He'd simply subdue any waves she made.

Justice smiled in satisfaction. It looked like he might have just found his apprentice/wife, and without any help from the computer. Just went to show that his intellect was more than a match for Pretorius's program. And wouldn't he take great pleasure in rubbing that fact in the old man's face.

Two

Daisy remained in her seat and waited while the line snaking toward the stage diminished. It would seem that everyone wanted a piece of Justice St. John and she wondered why. What had he done to inspire such effusiveness and excitement in the engineering world? Maybe she'd better research him when she returned home because, clearly, she was missing some vital information about her former lover.

The last individual reluctantly turned away and headed for the exit and in one lithe movement, Justice leaped from the stage and came straight for her. She wasn't surprised. She'd known from the first moment their eyes had met that he'd pursue her. For now, she'd let him.

"Would you care for a cup of coffee?" he asked.

She tilted her head to one side. Interesting. No wasted time. No social niceties. "Hello," she said and held out her hand. "Daisy Marcellus. It's a pleasure to see you again."

To her amusement that stopped him dead in his tracks and she could practically see the gears turning. "We've met before."

It wasn't a question so she didn't bother treating it like one, though part of her felt a stab of disappointment that her name didn't elicit more of a reaction. Or any reaction whatsoever. "You don't remember me, do you?"

"No."

Ah, that was the Justice she remembered. Blunt and to the point. "Maybe it'll come to you over coffee."

He folded his arms across an impressive expanse of chest. "Why don't you save us both time and refresh my memory?"

"I don't think I will. It's more fun this way."

"Fun." He said the word as though it left a nasty taste in his mouth.

She stood, startled to realize he'd picked up several inches in height along the way. When she'd known him, he'd been barely over six feet. He'd packed on at least three more inches in the ensuing years. "Yes, fun. As a noun, an amusement or playful activity. Alternately, the source of merriment. As an adjective, to give pleasure or enjoyment. As an intransitive verb, to play or joke." She grinned. "The mixed blessings of a photographic memory."

For some reason the admission allowed him to relax and he even managed a smile. A small one, but a smile nonetheless. "Thank you for the explanation. I wasn't familiar with the word."

"I'm shocked. How about *work?* Are you familiar with that word?"

He held up a hand before she could launch into a new set of definitions. "Quite familiar."

"Somehow that doesn't surprise me," she murmured.

"*Surprise.* Something unexpected that causes wonder or astonishment."

She chuckled, filled with wonder and astonishment at the unexpected sight of his laughing along with her. Impulsively, she caught his hand in hers. "I believe you said something about joining you for a cup of coffee?"

He stared at their linked fingers for a long moment. Then

he looked at her. Banked fire stirred in the brilliance of his gaze, a hunger and longing she couldn't mistake. Warmth filled her, splashing like hot liquid over and through her, sinking deep into her very core where it generated a hunger and longing as powerful as the one reflected in his eyes. From the moment he'd walked into her parents' home, he'd had the exact same effect on her. At least that much hadn't changed.

"Coffee would be an excellent start," he stated.

An excellent *start*? "And the finish?" she dared to ask.

"I think we both know the answer to that."

And she did. They would end up the same place they had the last time they'd been together.

In bed.

Hoping they wouldn't be interrupted by other conference attendees, Justice requested the hotel's café hostess show them to one of the more private tables buried toward the back and surrounded by greenery. It also happened to provide an impressive view across Biscayne Bay toward downtown Miami. The late afternoon rapidly transitioned toward dusk and the lights of the city flickered to life, the glow reflected in the soft blue water.

Daisy slid into the seat opposite Justice and he took the opportunity to study her. She was quite stunning, he acknowledged from a purely analytical standpoint, possessing features that society deemed beautiful. It didn't seem to matter whether he considered them each individually or took them in combination, they possessed an elegance in the same way he considered a carefully crafted mathematical formula elegant.

Her hair swept back from her brow to fall in a thick, straight line to cup her shoulders. Perhaps her left eyebrow was a tad off center, no more than a millimeter or two, but it only served to draw attention to the unusual green of her eyes, a shade that made him think of spring growth. Even more interesting, he could see every thought and emotion reflected there, her expression as open and ingenuous as a child. It disconcerted him since most female engineers were more guarded, perhaps as a result of working in such a male-dominated field.

He continued his appraisal. Her nose was much as a nose should be, straight and neither too narrow, nor too broad. Her cheekbones arched high, adding to that overall quality of elegance. As for her mouth… There, his gaze lingered. If she deviated from true classic beauty, it might be here. Her mouth was far more lush than elegant, full and a delicate pink. For some odd reason the shape and color made him want to bite it. Well, hell. That wouldn't do.

He cleared his throat. "So are you going to give me a hint?" he asked.

"I assume you mean you want a hint about where we met before?" Daisy asked, then shook her head in response to her own question. A tantalizing smile flirted with the corners of her mouth. Did she have any idea what that smile did to a man? The urge to bite grew stronger. "Give it time. It'll come to you."

"It might not." He frowned at the menu the hostess handed him and set it aside, unopened. He pushed the scientist in him to the fore, sliding into the reserved, analytical side of his nature with frightening ease. More and more he tended to retreat behind the facade whenever he found himself in an emotionally charged situation. He found it…safer. "I was in an accident six months and three-and-three-quarter days ago. Sometimes I struggle to recall names and certain events from my past."

She stared, shocked. "Oh, Justice, I'm so sorry. I had no idea."

"There's no reason you should since I worked quite hard to keep the general public from finding out." He hesitated. Maybe he should clarify. Women tended to appreciate that characteristic in a man. "Although it's caused a few memory issues, it hasn't affected my intellect, if that's of concern."

She caught his hand in hers and squeezed. "Don't be ridiculous. That's the least of my concerns."

He realized then that she was a touchy-feely type of woman. Unusual in an engineer, but he could live with it. Live with it? Hell, he could get used to it damn fast. He shrugged. "It's just one of those things you learn to accept. Sort of like the scars."

To his utter astonishment, tears pricked her eyes. "Oh, Justice. Scars?" She leaned toward him, speaking in a fierce undertone, her hand tightening on his. "Those don't matter, either. All they mean is that you're a survivor."

Another thought occurred. "We have the option of making love in the dark if you think the scars might have an adverse impact on your libido."

To his surprise, she burst out laughing. "Oh, thank goodness. I was afraid you'd changed. But you still have that marvelous sense of humor."

Did she think he was making a joke? He'd been dead serious. "Does that mean you're not interested in making love?" Maybe he should have led into the subject more gradually. But it seemed a logical progression, one that sandwiched quite neatly between coffee and asking her to be his apprentice/wife. "There's no rush. We have sixty-one hours and thirty-four minutes."

She laughed again, a light, carefree sound that arrowed straight to the icy core of him and thawed it ever so slightly. For the first time in years he felt the budding tendrils of hope. Maybe he wasn't a lost cause. Maybe winter would end. Maybe Daisy could deliver him into the warming arms of spring.

"I'm very interested in making love to you," she informed him. Her amusement faded, replaced by a bittersweet longing.

"It's been so long, Justice. I wish I'd thought to look for you sooner."

"You wouldn't have found me. Pretorius keeps us well hidden."

"Pretorius?"

"My uncle. He's a computer expert, which comes in handy since he helps maintain my anonymity."

"Huh." She fixed him with her lovely eyes, giving him her full attention and he realized he liked being the center of her universe. He liked it a lot. "I didn't realize you had any family. At least, you never mentioned anyone."

The way she spoke suggested they'd shared a certain level of intimacy. His eyes narrowed. Damn that accident. How could he have possibly forgotten someone like her? "How do I know you?"

She smiled. "Tell you what. I'll give you a hint. My appearance has changed quite a bit since we last met."

Aw, hell. Why did women always do that to a man? Normally, he was quite observant. But he rarely felt his observational abilities reached the level expected by women in male-female dynamics, particularly those of a romantic nature. "For instance?"

"My hair."

"Longer? Shorter?" He hazarded a guess, though guessing didn't come naturally to him.

She shook her head. "Lighter. It was a lot darker before. But I've gone back to my natural coloring."

Relief flowed over him like a comforting blanket. Okay, that explained it. No doubt the computer program disqualified her based on that minor detail. He'd have to speak to Pretorius about tweaking the parameters. Maybe he'd been a shade too rigid in his requirements.

"I could live with dark hair." Especially if it meant Daisy agreeing to become his apprentice/wife.

She tilted her head to one side, clearly puzzled by his comment. "Could you?"

Perhaps that sounded a trifle odd. Hadn't Pretorius warned him about inviting a woman for a cup of coffee in one breath and proposing to her in the next? Time to slow things down. After coffee he'd settle for propositioning her. She'd indicated a level of interest in pursuing that angle of their acquaintance, at least he hoped he'd made a correct interpretation of her interest. And if he were strictly honest with himself, if he didn't get her into bed soon he might give in to the temptation to bite more than just those lush lips of hers. He suspected such an action would be frowned upon given their current venue.

"Did we meet at a previous engineering conference?" he asked.

"Oh, I'm not—"

Their waitress appeared at his elbow and offered them a wide smile. "Good afternoon. My name is Anita and I'll be your waitress." She stated the obvious considering that she wore a uniform that clearly identified her occupation and her name tag had "Anita" written in bold black lettering. "Would you care for a drink from the bar?"

"I'll pass," Daisy said. "Though I'd love some iced tea, extra lemon please."

A sense of familiarity swept through Justice. Something about the extra lemon. And then it passed. The sensation happened all too frequently since the accident. Sometimes he couldn't summon the memory no matter how hard he tried. On other occasions—more and more often to his profound relief—the memory exploded into his mind in full vivid color, as though his brain had forged a new pathway through the neural wetware that held that precious information, avoiding the congestion and confusion left behind by his accident. But not this time. No matter how hard he tried to avoid it, he found himself square in the middle of a mental traffic jam, unable to maneuver his way to the coordinates that contained that particular node of memory.

He accepted the failure with his usual stoicism and switched his attention to the waitress. "Coffee. Black."

"I'll be right back with your drinks and to take your order."

The instant Anita left, Justice returned his attention to Daisy, homing in on her with laser-sharp focus. "Are you ready to give me another hint?"

She waved that aside. "I have a better suggestion. Why don't you tell me what you've been up to in the past few years? After all, you are the best in the business when it comes to creating robotic sensors and actuators."

They were on more familiar ground now. "Yes, I am."

"No false modesty, I see," she commented.

The observation made no sense. "What would be the point?"

He'd never met a woman who enjoyed laughing more than this one. He should find it annoying. Instead, it arrowed straight through him, bringing an unexpected surge of desire. "You crack me up, Justice. Still logical to the end."

He hesitated. "Is there something wrong with being logical?"

Everything about her seemed to soften, even her voice. "No, of course not. So long as you also remember to feel."

Feel? He didn't quite know how to respond to that, a rare occurrence and one that threw him off stride. He reached for Rumi, only to realize he'd left the sphere in his room. It also brought home to him how much he'd come to depend on his creation whenever he found himself in a quandary. And Daisy certainly left him in a quandary.

With most engineers, he knew exactly what to expect and how to speak to them. But not with this woman. Even her name seemed wrong, and yet... Right somehow. She had the same appeal as her namesake, a splash of color that brightened even the plainest, most barren landscape. She made him hesitate along his appointed path, encouraged him to pause in order to admire and while away the hours in ridiculous pursuits rather than the business of…well… business.

But it was more than that. She roused feelings in him he thought long dead, a want that eclipsed everything else. Right now sitting with her, he didn't give a damn about the conference, or the work he'd been unable to complete for the past year, or asking the necessary questions to ensure he'd found the perfect apprentice/wife. All he cared about was allowing spring to thaw the ice encasing his heart. To heat the blood flowing through his veins. To find the man lost in an endless winter and breathe new meaning into his life.

Daisy could do that for him. If he believed in intuition, he'd have blamed the abrupt, blazing certainty he experienced on that. But since he didn't, he decided his brain had been subconsciously working the problem and just now reached a rational and inescapable conclusion.

This woman was the answer to his problem.

He didn't question the newfound knowledge since he'd experienced something similar whenever he came up with a new idea in robotics. He'd learned to trust those moments of sudden enlightenment and proceed to the next step without delay.

She waited patiently for him to speak again, content with the silence. He found that an unusual attribute in a person, regardless of gender. While she waited, she smiled with what he interpreted as contentment and cupped her chin in the palm of her hand. She had pretty hands, he realized, the fingers long and supple. For an instant his brain short-circuited, and not as a result of his accident.

He flashed on an image of how Daisy's hands would look and feel on his body. Good God, where the hell had that come from? He wasn't normally the imaginative sort, and yet that one stunning picture caused an unmistakable physiological response, one far beyond his ability to control. No doubt because it had been so long since he'd been with a woman.

Something in his expression must have given him away. Daisy straightened in her chair. "Justice? What's wrong?"

He cleared his throat. "You'll have to forgive me. This hasn't happened since I was a teenager, but perhaps because of my recent isolation, I'm receiving an unusual amount of visually stimulating input which is having an adverse affect on my central nervous system. If you could strive to be a little less visually stimulating, my body will release an appropriate amount of nitric oxide to the *corpora cavernosa* which should cause my muscles to relax." Dear God, could he sound any geekier?

Sure enough, she blinked at him. "Excuse me?"

"You're giving me a hard-on."

The waitress chose that moment to return with their drinks and based on the unusual clumsiness with which she juggled her tray, he had a sneaking suspicion she'd overheard his final comment. Damn.

"Are you ready to order?" she asked, struggling in vain to maintain an impassive expression.

Justice didn't hesitate, but took the only reasonable course of action. "No. The check, please."

She handed it over, throwing a cynical look in Daisy's direction. For some reason that look stirred a fierce, protective instinct in Justice. Odd, since he didn't believe in instinct. The only explanation was some sort of genetic anomaly that had arbitrarily managed to survive the transition from an earlier, more primitive, intuitive state of man and been somehow included in his genetic coding.

Not that it mattered whether or not Daisy noticed Anita's reaction. Justice didn't want anyone looking at Daisy like that, thinking what the waitress was undoubtedly thinking, regardless of its veracity. Not that his soon-to-be-apprentice/wife noticed. She seemed totally oblivious to the byplay, probably because she was busy staring at him with undisguised shock. Maybe he should have been less blunt about his physiological problem.

Struggling to temper his reaction, he took the bill, added in a generous tip and slashed his signature across the ticket without his usual meticulous care. Then he shoved back his chair, relieved to discover that the nitric oxide had done its job.

Daisy's brows shot upward, a smile still playing at the corners of her mouth. "I gather we're leaving?"

"Yes. We're leaving."

She shrugged. "Okay."

She stood, snagged her carryall and slung the strap over her shoulder all in one fluid motion. The fuchsia of her bag should have clashed with the brilliant red of her blouse. Instead it made him think of the sunset that rapidly turned the Miami sky a similar color. Even the golden wheat shade of her hair seemed to add to the blend, intensifying his reaction to her.

Interesting. Perhaps he should consider researching the response of the human male's libido to the plumage choices of the female. He didn't know how he'd combine the results of the study in robotic design, but no doubt something would come to him in time. Until then, the only color he wanted to see was whatever shade Daisy turned when she was naked.

Before they'd progressed more than two feet, an elderly gentleman waylaid them. "Excellent speech, Mr. St. John. I particularly found your insights into future robotics and human interfacing quite fascinating."

Justice paused, taking the man's proffered hand. "Thank you. If you'll excuse me, we—"

Before he could whisk Daisy away, she spoke up, "He is the best on the planet when it comes to autonomous cooperation with humans."

"Very astute observation, young lady." His attention

returned to Justice. "I wonder if you'd have time to discuss an idea I had?"

Justice knew what would happen if he didn't get out of here and fast. It was the same thing that happened whenever engineers got together. They'd spend the entire night talking shop. Any other time, he'd have been happy to do just that. But not now. Not this night. Not when he hoped to spend it getting better acquainted with the woman he intended to transition into his apprentice/wife. Already he noticed surrounding ears and eyes perking up, could picture the gears turning, processors humming to life at the thought of an impromptu robotics discussion. Not a chance in hell.

"I have an appointment in precisely three minutes and forty-two seconds and it will take me exactly three minutes and thirty-three seconds to get there," he announced in a carrying voice. "If you'll excuse us?"

"Say no more." The man stepped hastily aside, as did the others who'd been in the process of approaching.

With the path clear, Justice settled his hand in the small of Daisy's back and ushered her through the crowd choosing a vector that afforded them the most direct route between their current location and the exit. The instant they stepped from the café, Daisy turned to confront him. She planted a hand square in the center of his chest, halting his forward momentum.

"What's going on?" she demanded.

Had he missed a step somewhere? "I thought you under-stood that part. Has there been a miscommunication?"

"You could say that. I probably wouldn't. Say it, I mean. I'd probably say something like, did we get our wires crossed?" She wrinkled her elegant nose. "Although even that sounds entirely too engineeringish."

Engineeringish? He folded his arms across his chest. "Would you prefer I be more direct?"

"No, you've been quite direct enough. I thought you invited me for coffee. What changed?"

He blew out a sigh. "I gather I should have allowed you to finish your iced tea before we proceeded to the next step?"

"Or maybe even have a single sip?" she teased. Instead of pushing against his chest, her hand lightened, shifted, driving him insane by making tiny, circular strokes. He had a sneaking suspicion that if she didn't stop—and soon—his body would use up its supply of nitric oxide. "I know we're attracted to each other. We always have been."

There it was again. That reminder that they knew each other from another time and place, a memory his accident must have stolen from him. "Have you changed your mind?"

"About making love to you?" She shook her head. "I just thought maybe we should slow down a little."

Yup. That nitric oxide needle was definitely shifting from *F* for Full to *E* for Empty. "I'm not sure I can," he confessed.

And it *was* a confession, since he found it difficult to admit to such a thing, and even more stunning to be experiencing what he regarded as a serious failing. Ever since he'd been in charge of his own life, he'd maintained ironclad control of his world and everything in it. Until then, he'd had no choice, no options, all decisions made around and to him regardless of the severity of their impact on him. The day he'd turned eighteen, he'd sworn that his life, how he spent it and who he allowed into it would be his decision and his alone.

Her eyes darkened, the spring green draped in deep forest shadow. "I can live without tea. How much time did you say we had until your next appointment?"

"There's ninety-four seconds left. But I lied about the appointment."

"Yes, I know. It's called a joke," she said gently. "In this particular use of the word, a noun. Meaning to cause laughter or amusement with one's words or actions."

"I'm not feeling laughter or amusement."

"No? What are you feeling?"

Feeling? He closed his eyes, a rush of adrenaline streaming through him. Heaven help him, she was right. After all this time, he was finally feeling. He struggled to identify the peculiar sensation.

"Hope," he whispered in a low, rough voice. "A verb used with or without attachment to an object. The anticipation, belief or trust that something greatly desired may at long last occur."

Daisy stared at Justice, her heart threatening to break. Did he have any idea how devastating she found his words? What had happened in those years they'd been apart that had altered him to the point where he'd gone so long without hope? Her hand fisted in his shirt and she tugged, drawing him closer.

"Take me to your room, Justice."

After all, what did it matter if she made love to him now or later? She'd known from the moment he'd swept onstage and their gazes had met and locked that this moment would come. They could sit in the trendy little café and drink coffee or tea until the sun set and stars spilled like fireflies across the velvety carpet of night sky. And it would only delay the inevitable.

She wanted him. She'd always wanted him. And despite the accident which had robbed him of some portion of his memory, part of him still knew her, still remembered how it had been between them. Because clearly, he wanted her, too. Spinning on her heel, she kept her hand anchored in his shirt and towed him toward the elevators.

"I gather we're leaving?" he asked in a dry voice, throwing her own words back at her.

"Yes. We're leaving."

He shrugged. "Okay. But just so you know, the elevators are in the opposite direction."

She didn't break stride, but simply reversed course. Was

that an actual smile she saw flash across his face? "And it didn't even crack," she informed him.

"Excuse me?"

"Your face when you smiled. I'm sure you'll be relieved to know that it didn't crack." This time when the smile came it was far broader and lingered longer. The sight filled her with intense satisfaction.

They arrived at the bank of elevators at the same moment that a set of doors opened, spilling passengers from its gilded innards. Entering the car, they stood in silence during the ride skyward, but Daisy could sense the growing tension between them, the bubble and simmer of it barely held in check, an explosion primed and ready to blow. The doors parted and Justice gestured to the right.

"Twenty-five-oh-one."

She waited by the door while he used his key card, then stepped inside, impressed by the size and beauty of his suite. "Wow."

"I like having both space and privacy. Since I was afforded neither during my formative years, I've found it holds greater value and appeal now."

"That doesn't surprise me." Daisy crossed to the expansive living area, one that looked out over a stunning view of the beach and ocean. "Who would have imagined we'd end up where we are now?" she murmured.

"I did. At least, in regard to my own future endeavors." His voice came from directly behind. Even though the comment sounded calm and prosaic—well, okay, and a trifle geeky— she could sense the desire seething just beneath the surface. "I had my life all planned."

"Yes, I suppose you did. You always were good at planning."

"It merely took determination combined with the right doors opening at the right time."

She threw him a smile over her shoulder. "Luck, Justice?"

He shook his head. "I don't believe in luck. I prefer to think of it as chance colliding with opportunity."

She chuckled, turning fully around to face him. "In other words…luck."

He lifted an eyebrow in inquiry. "Is it luck that you're here today?"

"Yes. Absolutely. If I hadn't seen your name advertised as the keynote speaker for the conference, I wouldn't be here now."

"But you did see it." He took a step in her direction, just one. But it was enough to kick her heart rate up a notch. "A door opened."

"And I decided to step through it." She spared a glance around. "Literally."

"As I said, chance combined with the right doors opening at the right time."

She gave a brisk nod and released her breath on a sigh. "So, tell me something, Justice. Now that you have me here, whatever will you do with me?"

He didn't answer right away, instead studying her with unnerving intensity. Had his expression always been so grave? He'd been quiet as a teen, studious, focused. But he'd also had the capacity to laugh. Where had that gone and how did she find it again?

He must have figured out what he intended to do with her because he took a final step in her direction. Hooking his index finger in the deep V of her blouse, he propelled her into his arms. She tumbled, just as she had all those long years ago, captured in an unbreakable hold.

"I believe I'm going to take off your clothes and make love to you," he informed her quite seriously.

And then he kissed her.

Three

Daisy slid her arms around Justice's neck and clung for all she was worth. She'd never appreciated methodical until this moment. But Justice managed to change her mind.

The first touch of his lips against hers came as an easy, tender caress. It stayed that way for a brief moment, just long enough for her to react. The instant she threw herself into the embrace, the tenor changed, became harder, more insistent. She sighed in delight, opening to him without hesitation or caution. He breached the seam of her lips, his tongue teasing hers, edging her hunger ever higher.

His control was exquisite, his taking decimating her. And then his teeth closed over her lower lip and tugged, threatening to drive her straight over the edge.

"You have no idea how long I've wanted to do that," he informed her.

It took Daisy a long moment to gather her wits sufficiently to respond to Justice's comment. "Not a clue. But I'm willing to bet you could tell me to the minute."

"To the nanosecond."

He cupped her face and practically inhaled her, his kiss the most thorough she'd ever received, his mouth firm and assured and potent. "Tell me what you want and I'll spend the rest of the night giving it to you."

It was all she could do to keep from moaning in response. "I was hoping you'd say that."

He smiled again, more easily this time. "Do you want the lights on or off when I remove your clothes?"

"Oh, yes."

Now he grinned. "Maybe I'll leave them off and see you wearing nothing but the sunset."

It was the most poetic comment he'd made since they'd become reacquainted and a cold place deep inside thawed, melted, warmed her, inside and out. "Then you'd better hurry because it's almost gone."

"I don't hurry. Not when it comes to something as important as this."

Daisy could only stare at him, helpless, a shaft of raw desire shooting through her. "Oh, Justice. I was so afraid."

"Afraid?" A frown creased his brow. "Of me?"

"In a way." She lifted a shoulder in a shrug and heard the happy clatter of children's toys rattling around in her carryall. The sound reassured her as nothing else could have. "Of how you'd be when I met you again. Whether you'd have changed. At first, I thought…"

"That I had?"

"How did you know?"

"It seemed the logical conclusion."

"Yes. I thought you'd changed." She swept the strap of her carryall from her shoulder and tossed the bag carelessly to the carpet. Fortunately, the contents stayed put, though they did jangle in protest. "And you have changed. It's natural, I suppose, since change is inevitable over time."

"An astute observation."

She couldn't help but laugh. "And yet, you're still the same. Underneath all the scientific jargon and aloofness, you're still the Justice I remember."

"I assume that's good?"

"It's…" For some reason tears pricked her eyes and she hastened to lower them, praying he hadn't noticed. She couldn't seem to contain her energy and plucked at one of the buttons on his black shirt. "It's fantastic," she admitted in a husky voice.

"Let's see if we can't make it even more fantastic."

Daisy had to admit, one of the qualities she'd always admired about Justice was his intense focus. He didn't waste further time talking, but applied his superb intelligence to shoving the buttons of her blouse through the corresponding holes. Sliding it from her shoulders, he neatly removed her bra with an experienced flick of his fingers.

What little remained of the setting sun bathed her in soft purpling shadows. His gaze followed the final traces of sunlight, while his hands painted her in heat. He cupped the weight of her breasts and slid his thumbs across the tips. His hands surprised her with their power and strength. They weren't the soft hands of a pencil pusher, but those of a laborer, callused and hard. Whatever sort of engineering and robotic work he did involved the use of those hands, his efforts strengthening and defining their shape and texture. She moaned at the delicious abrasiveness, her knees threatening to give out beneath her.

"Justice, please."

"Don't ask me to rush this. I can't. I won't. I want to enjoy every moment."

Despite his demand, his hands reluctantly slid from her breasts across her quivering abdomen. The sound of the zipper of her slacks being lowered sounded as harsh as their breathing. He skinned the last of her clothing from her body, leaving her cloaked in nudity.

It was Daisy's turn to return the favor. She didn't have

Justice's patience, nor his attention to methodical process. She yanked and tugged whatever came to hand, whether trousers or shirt or shoes and socks. While darkness enclosed them in a soft fist, she allowed her hands to be her eyes while she reacquainted herself with every inch of him.

So much had changed. Not only was he taller, but broader. More heavily muscled. Deliciously ridged and toned. She'd love to paint him like this, to capture not only the incredible maleness of him, but that essence of intellect combined with potent masculinity.

Her hand glanced off a ridge that wasn't muscle, a long slashing tear across smooth skin. "Oh, Justice. You weren't kidding about the scars, were you?"

He stiffened. "It should be too dark for you to see."

"Well, yes. But I can feel it."

"Do you find it offensive? Would you prefer to terminate our lovemaking?"

"Termin—" Daisy smothered a laugh. "Honestly, Justice. You're so funny. I can always tell when you're upset. You start talking in Basic Geek."

"I'm not upset."

"Then what are you?"

"I'm…" He released his breath in a long sigh. "I'm emotionally compromised."

"It would be a little surprising if you weren't," she informed him gently. He didn't reply, but remained still and quiet beneath her tentative touch. Did he think she'd walk away because of a few scars? He didn't know her very well anymore, but he'd soon learn. "Let me show you how offensive I find your scars."

Ever so gently, her touch as soft and light as the sweep of butterfly wings, she pressed her lips to the first, tracing it from end to end. She located the next one and kissed that one, as well. And the next, until she'd found each and every one, created a road map of lingering caresses across his body.

"No more." His harsh voice split the silence, as twisted and tortured as his scars.

He swept her into his arms and carried her through the living area into the bedroom. A single light burned a pathway through the darkness, chasing away the shadows and haloing the bed in a ring of gold. He came down beside her and the warm glow skated over his work-hardened muscles and sank into the crevices lining his face. Pain lingered there, a pain she'd have given anything to ease. And maybe she could.

Daisy reached for him, pulled him into the warmth of her embrace and adjusted her curves to accommodate his lean, graceful form. No question, Justice had become the panther she'd long considered him, sleek and trim, with an edge of tough, masculine danger. His skin rippled beneath her touch, the sweep of warm, taut sinew as appealing to the artist within her as the faint golden hue of his skin tones. His hardness pitted against all that made her yielding and feminine, creating an interesting dichotomy, one she could lose herself in. So why resist?

This time when she mapped the pathway of scars, she did it within that merciless glare of light. She wished her kisses had the power to heal, that she could give ease and comfort to the rips and tears that had damaged not just his body, but somehow his heart and soul, as well. She anointed each and every one while he lay rigid beneath her, his jaw rigid and eyes squeezed shut.

She had an instant's warning before he moved, the quick clench and flex of toned muscle. And then he had her flat on her back, his arms planted on either side of her head, caging her. He held himself above her, his gaze marking her like a hot branding touch.

"My turn," he said.

Not giving her an opportunity to reply, his mouth closed over hers, hungry with demand and intent. Sheer pleasure swamped her and she wrapped her arms around his neck, tugging him down until all of him blanketed her in endless masculinity. With a husky laugh that turned her insides molten, he slid his hands between them and traced her breasts, exploring every inch, shaping them, dragging those delicious calluses over and around before lowering his head to catch one taut tip between his teeth. Her breath escaped, sharp as an explosion while pleasure ripped through her.

"Justice…" His name escaped on a cry, blurred with passion. "Do that again."

The last time she'd been held in his arms, had known his possession, it had been gentle and sweetly tender. Tentative. They'd been little more than children, filled with an insatiable curiosity and delight in the physical, yet cautious in that exploration.

This time, it was so much more, their knowledge deeper, their desires fine-tuned. And they were far from children. In all the years that separated the two occasions, one thing hadn't changed. The magic still existed between them. At his first touch, he revived some inexplicable connection between them that strengthened and intensified with each passing moment.

Justice's hand slid from her breasts and drifted ever lower until he'd found the welcoming warmth at the apex of her thighs. He dipped inward, a stroking touch, easing her legs apart until she lay spread beneath him, fully open to his gaze. The muscles of her belly and thighs rippled with pleasure, the feeling intensifying with each slow movement of his fingers. He took his time, driving her insane with his thoroughness. Heaven help her, but she adored thorough men.

"Please, Justice. I can't take any more."

"I hope you can take more, since I have plenty to give you." Again, he treated her to that soft, husky laugh. So deep. So dark and delicious. So intimate. She heard the slide of a bedside table drawer followed by the muted rip and crackle of a wrapper. With swift, economical movements, he protected himself. "Let me give you everything I have, Daisy."

She groaned, her breath quickening, just as her body quickened, tightening with a desire so intense she thought she'd die from it. He levered himself above her, cupping her bottom and lifting her. He came down heavily, dipping into her liquid heat.

With one slow stroke, he surged into her, filling her with steely power. She wrapped her arms and legs around him, angled her hips to take him more deeply. She wanted it to last forever, to cling to this moment and revel in it. Never had she experienced anything like this, not with anyone other than him. She didn't understand it, didn't need to understand. She simply embraced it and rejoiced.

And then she couldn't think, could only crack and splinter while she rode the storm with him, fragmenting into endless pieces as she embraced the wildness that exploded from beneath his impeccable control. With every thrust he sent her flying toward ecstasy, driven higher and further than she'd ever been driven before.

It was a transcendent moment she'd only experienced once before and with only one man. This man. These arms. This same joining, even if years apart. Did he feel it? Did he sense the connection they'd forged once again? Did he realize what she did? She'd thought by having this night together that she'd finally be able to let her memories of him go. Instead, she'd discovered something far different.

Somehow, despite all odds, they'd become one, and there would be no going back. From this moment on, she belonged to him, just as he belonged to her. And they always would.

Nighttime wheeled by. Justice ordered food that remained uneaten. Started sentences that broke off, unfinished. Drew a bath that turned cold, forgotten. Instead, they tumbled into each other's arms, insatiable. At some point they slept.

He only knew it with any certainty because somehow night became day.

He woke with a slow smile and a bone-deep certainty that his life had taken a turn, had shifted from one plane to another, and there'd be no going back. Not that he had any interest in going back.

He glanced down at Daisy where she slept like the dead, curled against him so tightly they practically shared the same skin. She'd pillowed her head on his shoulder, her hair a tormenting sweep of silk against his chest. Her hand was splayed there, as well, her palm dead center over his heart, as though she gathered up every beat, absorbing it until it became one with her own.

So what next? How did he convince her to become his apprentice/wife? Because he had no intention of letting her go.

Gently, lovingly, he eased out from beneath her. Lifting up on one elbow, he traced the velvety length of her from shoulder to breast, waist to hip to the pert curve of her bottom. And that's when he saw it, resting right behind her left hip. A tattoo peeked out at him, a pair of golden eyes gleaming from behind deep green leaves.

The memory exploded in his head, so ripe with pain it might have occurred only minutes ago. His foster home. What should have been his last placement. For the first time since he'd been orphaned, this one had been a real home, not like the endless stream of residences where he'd been one of a pack. The unwanted. The forgotten. The neglected. The rejected.

This was a true home with loving parents, his own room... and Daisy. Her name scorched his brain with tongues of fire, ripping through the misty veil of forgetfulness caused by his accident and he remembered, remembered it all. The Marcellus residence had been a summertime way station between his senior year in high school and his first semester at Harvard. He wasn't the only foster child, and yet the Marcelluses had somehow juggled family interests with work with caring for the needs of those they took in. It would have been perfect, except...

Except for Daisy.

The moment he'd walked into his new home and seen her at the bottom of a pile of foster rugrats, he'd wanted her. He shouldn't have, not considering she'd sported spiky Goth-black hair, kohl-rimmed green eyes and purple-tipped finger- and toenails. He'd been so used to people judging without knowing him, that he tried never to make the same mistake. And it only took one look to see straight through to the sweetness beneath the outer craziness. Or what he thought was sweetness.

Instead, she'd lied to him from beginning to end.

Justice escaped the bed in one fluid movement and crossed the room. Ripping open the closet, he snagged the first pair of slacks that came to hand and yanked them on, struggling for control. Damn it to hell, where had his control gone? It had always been like that with her. She possessed an uncanny knack for pushing the exact right buttons guaranteed to turn his carefully laid plans inside out and upside down.

"Justice?" Her sleepy voice came from the warmth of the bed, slow and sweet and contented. And oh, so false.

He snatched a deep breath. Then another. His temper might be held by a tenuous thread, but at least it held. He turned and faced her. "Good morning."

She blinked the sleep from jade-green eyes, focusing in on him. "What's wrong?"

"Nothing. I'd like you to leave now."

She sat up in bed. Her hair should have been snarled and knotted with snakes, like Medusa's head. Instead, the wheat-blond length tumbled straight as a waterfall to her shoulders. The sheet dipped toward her waist exposing the lovely apple-breasts he'd found so unbearably sweet last night. In the morning light, he could see the nipples were rosy pink, the same rosy pink as the color sweeping across her cheekbones.

It didn't make sense to him. She was a snake in the grass. An asp posed to strike. And yet, he didn't think he'd ever seen a more beautiful sight. How was that possible?

She blinked those impossibly green eyes at him. "I'm sorry. Did…did you just ask me to leave?"

"Yes."

Good. Short and to the point. No mistaking the response, either. She was a woman. They tended to take longer to dress and do whatever it was women did in the morning. He ran a fast calculation. Chances were excellent that she'd be gone in just under nine-point-four minutes.

"There is something wrong. What is it?"

She shot from the bed and seeing her in the sunlight, every inch of her on full display, nearly brought Justice to his knees. No question. If he survived the next nine-point-three minutes it would be a miracle. And he didn't believe in miracles.

"I remember who you are."

"You do?" She smiled in delight. "That's great. How did you figure it out?"

"Your tattoo." That damnable tattoo. "Seeing it has somehow forged a connection between my consciousness and that particular set of memories."

"Was that all it took?" She had the nerve to laugh. "I'm surprised your own tattoo didn't do that."

"I don't have a tattoo."

"Sure you do. A panther's paw with claw marks to match my cat's eyes." She pointed. "It's there on your hip—" She broke off, distress causing her to catch her lower lip between her teeth, a lip he'd taken great delight in catching between his own teeth only hours earlier. "Oh, Justice. There's only a scar there now. I'm so sorry."

"Stop it, Daisy." He cut her off with a slice of his hand.

"Your tattoo is merely a catalyst. I don't just remember who you are. I also remember what you did."

"What I did?"

A tiny line formed between her brows. Excellent. Maybe it would encourage wrinkles to form and she'd be less appealing. Of course, that might take thirty years. Or even fifty, depending on her genetics. He didn't think he could wait that long. He needed her out *now*.

"You lied about your age that summer. You told me you were seventeen. You told me you would be a high school senior to my college freshman, just one year behind me. Instead, you were a fifteen-year-old child."

"Almost sixteen," she retorted, stung. "And I lied because I knew you wouldn't kiss me if I told you the truth."

"Kiss you?" The thread holding his temper snapped. He literally heard it, the sound as loud and sharp as the crack of a whip. He came at her, not even realizing he moved until he caught her shoulders in his hands and yanked her onto her toes. "I made love to you. You were a damn virgin. You were…untouchable and I touched you. The one true home I'd had since my parents died and you ruined it for me. Took it from me. I lost my scholarship because of you because I was no longer of 'good character.'" Dear God that had hurt. Devastated. "Because of you Harvard wouldn't touch me."

"What?" He couldn't mistake the shock on her face. Nor could she have faked the way every scrap of color drained from her face and the pupils of her eyes narrowed to pinpricks. "Oh, Justice. I'm so sorry. They told me you'd left early for college… I never realized…"

He released her and stepped away. "Put on your clothes."

That brought color back to her face. Without a word, she snatched up the various bits and pieces scattered across the suite and dressed. Even that she did with grace and elegance, and Justice turned his back, unable to watch without— Without wanting her again. Without touching her again.

Without snatching her into his arms, carrying her to that bed and making love to her until they were both too exhausted to move. How the hell could he still want her after what she'd done?

"Justice?"

He hadn't heard her approach, but he sure as hell felt her tentative touch on his bare arm. He almost broke, catching himself at the last instant. He turned on her, wanting her to understand just how much she'd cost him. How he'd never forgive her duplicity.

"That final home, that *place*—" he practically spit out the word "—they put me those final months was the worst of them all. They knew what I'd done and treated me..." He broke off, shaking his head, his back teeth clamping as he fought back the blistering spill of emotions. Emotions he refused to acknowledge. Refused to allow to touch him ever again. "When I turned eighteen, they kicked me loose. I had nowhere to go, no one to help me. No job or money and no chance of acquiring either."

Her breath hitched throughout his recital, disbelief warring with... It took him a moment to identify the emotion. Pain? Heartbreak? "I didn't know. I swear I didn't."

Tears came then, sliding down her cheeks and reddening her eyes and nose. She wasn't a pretty crier. Instead of pleasing him, the discovery bothered him on some deep, visceral level, perhaps because it suggested that her tears were sincere. He should have taken pleasure in her distress, felt some sort of redemption. Once upon a time he might have. But not now. Not after all these years. He struggled to ignore the tears, using her emotion to lock away his own. To distance himself from that long-ago time.

"Are you even an engineer?" he demanded.

"No, of course not."

Of course not? God save him from illogical women. "You are at an engineering conference. Only engineers were permitted to attend the keynote speech. No guests. No media. No—" He made an impatient gesture. "Whatever you are."

"I write and illustrate children's storybooks."

It was so far out of expectation that it took him a split second to adjust his thinking. "Then, what the hell were you doing at my speech?"

"I saw your name and photograph on one of the hotel placards and recognized you. I slipped in on impulse."

"You told me you were an engineer."

She scrubbed impatiently at her cheeks before planting her hands on her hips. "I most certainly did not. In fact, I told you I wasn't."

He sorted through their time together and came up empty. "No, you didn't."

"It was when we had tea. Or rather, didn't have tea." She drove that point home with pinpoint accuracy. "You asked if we'd met at an engineering conference and I said I wasn't an engineer." She hesitated. Blushed. "Well, to be honest—"

"Yes, please. I'm sure it would make a nice change for you."

Anger flickered to life in her gaze. "I never lied to you. I told you we'd met before. I never claimed to be an engineer. In fact, I started to explain what I did for a living when the waitress arrived. If she hadn't interrupted, I'd have been able to finish my sentence. By the time she left, the conversation switched gears." She folded her arms across her chest. "As I recall, you asked me for another hint."

"Maybe you should have told me you were the woman who ruined my chance to attend Harvard. That would have been an excellent hint."

"I'm sorry. I had no idea." Her apology sounded sincere, not that it helped.

Even so, he caught the distress and pain. Not on her own account, but for him. Not that he wanted it. "They could have pressed charges against me. Your parents threatened to."

"If they'd pressed charges I would have told the authorities the truth. That I lied to you about my age and what happened between us was consensual. Quite consensual," she made a point of adding, then released a sigh heavy with regret. "I swear to you, Justice, I didn't know they'd found out. They never told me. I just woke up one day and you were gone."

"And that would have made everything all right? Damn it to hell, Daisy. I took you to a tattoo parlor—" Another thought struck him and he groped on the dresser for Rumi, his fingers fumbling across the smooth surface. "Son of a bitch. I let you drive to the tattoo parlor."

She reddened. "I was a bit…precocious back then."

"Precocious?" he roared. "You were a walking, talking bundle of rampaging hormones intent on getting into as much trouble as possible, while dragging me along for the ride."

"That, too." Her expression turned wistful. "But it was fun while it lasted, wasn't it?"

"Out." He couldn't take another minute without totally losing his temper. What was it about her that drove him so close to the edge? "I want you to leave. Now."

"For what it's worth, Justice, I really am sorry. I never realized you paid such a steep price for something so wonderful."

"It wasn't wonderful for me."

"No," she whispered. "I guess not. Just like last night wasn't wonderful, either."

"It was sex."

She flinched and he realized he'd hurt her. Really hurt her. She moistened her lips and gave a curt nod. "Of course. Well, thanks for the amazing sex, Justice."

Without another word, she turned and left the bedroom and his only thought was that she considered their sexual encounter amazing. He wasn't sure any of his previous partners had ever called it amazing. It shouldn't matter, and yet somehow it did. He heard her rummage around in her carryall for endless moments, the contents clashing and chattering in agitation. Then silence. What the hell was she doing? Because he knew damn well she hadn't left. He could still *feel* her. And that alone threatened to drive him insane. Finally, finally, finally, the suite door opened and closed behind her.

He released his breath in a long sigh. Okay, she was gone, this time for good. It might have taken fourteen-point-six minutes instead of the nine plus he'd originally calculated, but at least the confrontation was behind him. He headed for the living area and crossed to the phone, intent on alerting the front desk of his early departure. Sitting on the desk he found a book that hadn't been there before. A children's storybook. He set Rumi aside and reached for the book, hesitating at the last minute.

The cover exploded with color, teeming with plants and flowers that seemed to overrun the jacket. It took his eyes a moment to adjust to the chaotic riot of shape and shade. Then the analytical side of his brain kicked in and he began to separate the various objects, leaf from bud, fruit from flower, until finally he caught the intense gold eyes peering through the jungle foliage, their appearance almost identical to her tattoo.

The eyes were also eerily familiar, maybe because he looked at them every damn day in the mirror.

He touched the cover, tracing the bit of black panther she'd buried within the scene. Unable to help himself, he opened the book. She'd autographed it with her first name and a swift sketch of a flower—a daisy, of course. *"To Justice,"* she wrote. *"I got it wrong. You're not Cat."*

The words didn't make any sense to him until he leafed through the pages and discovered that she'd named the panther Cat. Beside the huge jungle cat romped a domesticated kitten named Kit. She was a tabby, one with green eyes and wheat-blond stripes, identical in name and appearance to the kitten he'd given Daisy the day they'd made love. He'd chosen the silly creature because it reminded him of her. He'd even tied a huge floppy green bow around its neck, one that had been half-shredded by the time he'd presented Daisy with the kitten.

Unable to resist, Justice flipped the book to the beginning and read more carefully this time. He quickly realized this was the first in a series of books about the adventures of Kit and Cat, and told the tale of a kitten lost in the jungle who meets a panther cub. The two became best friends. Kit caused nothing but trouble and Justice found himself smiling since it was so similar to the sort of escapades Daisy used to get into. But Cat was always there to rescue her, to protect her from the dangers of the jungle. Even when it meant choosing between her and his pride, Cat faithfully remained by Kit's side.

He flipped the book closed and his glance fell on Rumi. Somehow, at some point during his argument with Daisy, he'd transformed the sphere. It sat on the desk, its ebony pieces gleaming in the sunlight, the mathematical symbols flowing symmetrically across the metallic petals of the flower he'd created.

A daisy.

Justice's hands balled into fists and he took a step back, rejecting both creations—book and flower. He wasn't Cat any more than she was Kit. Even more telling, she'd made a mistake in the book. Didn't she know? Hadn't she researched her facts? Panthers didn't have prides.

Panthers were loners.

Four

Nineteen months, fifteen days, five hours,
nineteen minutes and forty-three seconds later...

Daisy jiggled the tiny earbud that never seemed willing to fit properly in her ear. "Are you sure you have the directions right, Jett?" she asked the girl she'd agreed to foster nearly a year earlier.

"Positive," came the breezy retort.

With an exclamation of disgust, Daisy pulled off the pavement and onto the narrow shoulder. A harsh November wind swept by, causing the small compact rental to shudder from the blast. This time of year never failed to depress her. It was an in-between season that offered neither the crisp and glorious richness of fall, nor the deep, frosty slumber of full winter. Instead, it hovered somewhere in the middle, a twilight that was neither a beginning nor an end, not a becoming nor a final metamorphosis.

She snagged the map from the passenger seat and fought

through the various fanlike folds to spread it open across the steering wheel, even though she could picture every road and turn in perfect detail from the last time she'd checked it. Sure enough, her memory hadn't failed her. None of the various lines and squiggles included the turnoff for the homestead Jett had described.

"Listen up, Jett," Daisy announced. "I'm lost in the wilds of Colorado. This place isn't on the map and your stupid GPS is demanding I make a U-turn at my earliest convenience and leave. I'm inclined to do what she suggests."

"Dora is an idiot," Jett announced cheerfully.

"I believe I told you that when you insisted I take her."

"She's still young. Give her time to mature."

Daisy choked on a laugh. "*She's* young? That's rich, coming from you."

"I'm sixteen and eight months, or I will be tomorrow. Dora is eleven months and three days, the exact same age as Noelle."

Daisy flinched at Jett's precision. Even though there was no biological relationship, her comment was so like Justice. When would she get over it? When would those little reminders finally stop bothering her? Never. That's when.

As impossible as it seemed, she'd fallen in love with Justice when she'd been little more than a child and had been devastated when he'd disappeared without a word of explanation. Without even saying goodbye. She'd mourned for years, searched for him for years, the constant hope dancing in her heart that he'd somehow find his way back to her. So strong was the hope that she refused to form any other attachments until her junior year at college. To her intense disappointment that relationship had never matched what she'd experienced with Justice.

And then a miracle had happened and she'd found him again. Despite the fact that they'd only shared a single night together, this latest parting had been far worse, perhaps because they'd bonded on an adult level. Or so she'd thought. For those few short hours she'd opened herself completely to him, just as she had as a teenager. Allowed herself to believe that he'd connected as deeply and utterly as she had.

If it hadn't been for her daughter, she didn't know how she'd have gotten through the past year and a half. And now that it had become apparent that Noelle shared her father's brilliance, Daisy had tracked Justice down to the bitter ends of the earth. Though Jett didn't realize it, the brazen teen reminded her of him, as well, possessing both his keen intellect in addition to his meticulous nature. Of course, she also reminded Daisy of herself at that age—creative, a bit outrageous, brash, and pure trouble waiting to happen.

Daisy set her jaw, thinking about the coming confrontation with Justice. Somehow, someway, she needed to harden herself against her emotions. To shut them off as cleanly as he had. She couldn't risk tumbling a third time. She didn't think she'd survive it.

"Okay, Jett. Let's get this done," Daisy announced. "Now where am I and how do I get to Justice? Because from what I can see, there's nothing out here for a billion miles."

"That's quite a feat considering the circumference of the earth is only 24,901.55 miles. That's at the equator. If you're referring to the circumference from pole to pole—"

Daisy's back teeth clamped together. "You know what I mean."

Jett had initially been her parents' foster child. She'd still be one, if the Marcelluses hadn't withdrawn from the program due to her father's heart attack. When he'd become ill, Jett begged Daisy to take the required steps necessary to foster her since the two had struck up a firm friendship. Fortunately, Daisy's storybook series had been a huge hit, one that provided the sort of royalty checks enjoyed by only an elite few, enabling her to live her life as she saw fit, including fostering a precocious teenager. That had been ten months ago and they'd discovered to their mutual delight that the arrangement worked well for them both.

"Okay, listen and obey," Jett instructed. "Drive precisely three-point-two miles south from your current location. There will be a dirt road on your left. Turn down it. Continue on for another ten-point-nine miles. If you still don't see anything, call me."

"And one more thing... How do you know where I am?"

"Dora told me."

Daisy sighed. "Tattletale."

"Noelle and I are following your GPS signal, aren't we, Red?"

Daisy caught the happy babble of her daughter's voice slipping across the airwaves and found herself missing her baby more than she thought possible. It was the first time she'd left Noelle for an extended period of time and she found the separation beyond distressing.

She put the car in gear and pulled out onto the pavement. "I'll call you when I get there."

"We'll be waiting."

An undercurrent of excitement threaded through Jett's voice. Ever since she discovered Daisy actually knew The. Great. Justice. St. John. and more impressive, he was Noelle's father, Jett had worked nonstop to uncover his lair. At least, that's how Daisy thought of it, considering he kept his location so well hidden. Heaven knew, she'd never been successful at locating him. And she had tried.

The minute she'd discovered she was pregnant, she'd spent a full year and a half attempting to track him down with zero success. She'd sent endless letters through every engineering source she could think of, again with zero success. It had taken Jett precisely one month. Okay, twenty-nine days, eleven hours, fourteen minutes and a handful of seconds. The teenager had noted the exact time in her final progress report.

Which brought Daisy to her current location and task…to snare the elusive panther in his equally elusive den.

The fourteen-point-whatever mile drive took nearly an hour. Daisy couldn't help but think the rutted road, one that threatened to break both axles, as well as shake loose most of her teeth, was a deliberate attempt on Justice's part to keep unwanted visitors from accidentally stumbling across him. Because, sure enough, the instant Dora's mileage indicator hit the combined distance of surface and dirt roads Jett had decreed, Daisy crested a hill and found a huge complex sprawled beneath her, blending so beautifully into the surrounding meadow that it almost looked like a mirage.

Brigadoon rising from the mists of time.

She put through a call to Jett. "I'm here."

"I found it? For real?" Jett practically squealed in excitement, sounding for the first time in a long time like a typical teenager, something she definitely was not. *"Yes!"*

"You're pumping your fist, aren't you?"

"Yes!"

"I'll call you after my meeting."

"I want it word for word."

"I have a photographic memory, not audiographic, but I'll do my best."

Daisy removed the earbud and switched it off. Shoving the car in gear, she rolled down the hillside toward what appeared to be a ranch complex, complete with barn, paddock, pastures, homestead and even a windmill. Despite that, a vague sensation of emptiness hung over the place, as though time held its breath. Rolling to a stop in front of the sprawling house, she switched off the engine and sat, fighting for calm.

All during the lengthy process of tracking Justice down, she'd shied away from considering how she'd deal with "the moment" when they finally came face-to-face. What would she say? How would he react? Would he even care that she'd given birth to their daughter?

Or would he say something clever like, "Fascinating," and then go invent more robotic whatzit sensors and cooperating actuators with autonomous humans, or whatever he was the best on the planet at doing. Not that it mattered. So long as he acknowledged his daughter, acknowledged his responsibility in her creation and supplied their baby with what she needed, Daisy didn't really care what he did or where he did it.

So. This was it.

She eyed the wide front porch and gnawed on her lower lip. No more procrastinating. Time to beard the mad scientist in his secret lab. Smacking her palm against the steering wheel for emphasis, she shoved open the door to the rental car, climbed out and slammed it closed. Marching up the steps to the front porch, she crossed to the entryway. Something about it struck her as odd and it took a moment to realize what.

No windows in or around the door.

No handle.

No doorbell or knocker.

Damn.

Balling up her fist, she pounded on the thick oak barricade. "Justice? Justice St. John? I want to talk to you."

Nothing.

She gave the door a swift kick for extra emphasis. "I'm not leaving, Justice. Not until we talk."

Not a sound. Not a reaction of any kind. It was as though the house slept. Daisy shivered. Almost like it was caught in some other moment in time or an alternate universe. Another dimension, maybe, like Brigadoon. Maybe it wasn't time for them to wake up, yet.

Or maybe he simply wasn't home.

She paced in front of the door, wondering what she should do next. And that's when she noticed another oddity about the doorway, a reflective gleam buried in the trim work. She paused in her pacing and studied the anomaly. Son of a gun.

A camera. Someone was watching and she'd bet her next four impressively large royalty checks she knew who it was.

Well, now. Wasn't that interesting? She might stink at math, but she could solve this particular equation. She'd found the God of Geekdom hiding in an unmarked valley in Colorado, buried behind thick walls with a door but no handle, the place as unwelcoming as he could make it. Oh, she could add up those numbers to equal…

She marched straight up to the camera and tilted her face so she could glare directly at the tiny circle of glass. "Justice? You either open this door or I'm going to get on the phone and call every media source I can think of and tell them where you live. And then I'm going to get on the internet and post the location on every geek-site I can find."

An instant later the front door emitted a persnickety click and eased inward a fraction. Daisy gave it a shove, not the least surprised when it opened to her touch. She stepped across the threshold into a chilly gloom that left her squinting. The door swung closed behind her and the dead bolt slammed home with a rifle-sharp retort, locking her inside.

"If that's meant to scare me, you didn't succeed," she announced. Then in an undertone, "Intimidated me a little bit, maybe, but you didn't scare me."

Daisy glanced around the foyer, struggling to get a good look at her surroundings. Difficult, considering the lack of natural light. What was the deal with windows around here? The cold air contained a stale, dusty quality, as though the area was rarely used. Justice certainly hadn't wasted any of his trillions heating this section of his homestead and she shivered in the confines of her thin coat, missing the Florida warmth and sunshine.

She took another step into the dimness. Without any carpeting to absorb the sound, the impact of her shoes against the slate flooring bounced in noisy protest off the featureless walls. She looked around, curiosity combining with nervousness. The huge entranceway lacked the usual bits and pieces most foyers contained. No tables or racks or mirrors or pictures or freestanding artwork. Just…emptiness. Well, and dust. She turned in a slow circle looking for a light switch and coming up empty. Okay, that was just weird.

What little she could see through the gloom of the surrounding rooms spoke of huge expanses of space as stark and empty as the foyer, though she could see their potential in the flow and symmetry of the overall structure. She particularly liked the liberal use of wood, not to mention the fact that the other rooms had honest-to-goodness windows, even if they were shuttered. Why in the world would he live in such a magnificent home and keep it closed up and empty? It didn't make any sense.

Before she could work up the nerve to explore, she caught the hard clip of boots ringing against floorboards, the sound echoing through the painful emptiness. The footsteps moved in her direction at a steady, unhurried pace. For some reason that firm, deliberate tread added to the intimidation factor, his coming an inescapable certainty.

No turning back now.

A moment later his impressive form filled a doorway to her right, one draped in dense shadow. Everything inside of her blossomed to life, responding to the man instinct told her was Justice, even though she couldn't see him clearly. She closed her eyes, fighting against an almost overpowering urge to race toward him and throw herself into his arms. To allow all she kept bottled inside to burst free, like spring sunshine burning away the ice damming a river's reckless flow.

"How did you find me, Daisy?" His cold voice cut through the darkness with knifelike sharpness, confirming his identity. Not that she had any doubt.

She sighed. How like him to skip over the social niceties. "Hello, Justice. I'm fine, thanks. Yes, it's been a long drive. Why, yes, I'd love something to drink."

He didn't respond immediately. And then, "You threatened to expose me to the media."

"You wouldn't let me in. It was the only leverage I had." This was ridiculous. She crossed the foyer toward him, feeling the bond between them tighten and ensnare her with each step she took. "Come on, Justice. Get us something to drink and let's sit down and talk. It's important."

The closer she came the more clearly she could see him. Dear heaven, but he'd changed during the months they'd been apart. An icy remoteness cascaded off of him in frosty waves. He'd become harder, more self-contained than ever. What had happened to cause such a change?

She didn't dare touch him. No point in risking frostbite, though part of her longed to. "Are you all right?" she asked in concern.

"No."

Another thought occurred, a horrifying thought. "Oh, Justice, are you ill?"

"My health is perfect, thank you."

Then what in the world had happened to him? She stiffened. He couldn't have turned into this glacial, winter-bound man as a result of their encounter at the engineering conference. In order for that to be the case, their night together would have had to mean something to him, impacted his life in some way. And though it broke her heart to admit it, she'd long ago come to the conclusion that those glorious hours had meant nothing to him. Less than nothing. Otherwise he'd have tracked her down. At the very least he'd have responded to the endless letters she'd sent him.

He lifted an eyebrow. "You wanted something to drink before you left?"

Daisy released her breath in a sigh. This was going to be even harder than she'd anticipated. "I would, yes."

Justice led the way down a wide hall into a huge, impressive kitchen that looked like something out of a futuristic movie, though it seemed to be missing the normal collection of appliances. "Lights," he requested and instantly a bank of recessed lighting flared to life.

She stared in wonder, impressed. "Is that how you turn on the lights around here?"

"Yes, if your voice is coded for computer authorization." He paused a beat, his smile set well below frigid. "Which, yours is not. Water, tea, pop or something stronger?"

"Water's fine." She swiped her hands along the sides of her jeans, fighting nerves. "I wouldn't have told, you know. Where you live, I mean," she added for clarification.

He tapped a swift code onto a black glass plate affixed to the wall. With a soft hiss a pair of bottles slid out from a slot in the wood paneling. He handed her one, the temperature so cold her fingers went instantly numb. Twisting off the lid of the other, he stared at her while he took a long swallow. "I know you wouldn't have told anyone," he said.

"Really?" For some reason his certainty pleased her and she relaxed enough to smile. "How do you know?"

"Because Pretorius has jammed your cell signal. And he'll continue to jam it until I tell him otherwise."

Her smile faded. "When do you intend to tell him otherwise?" she asked warily.

"As soon as my uncle and I relocate. Until then, you'll remain here as our guest."

She paused with the bottle halfway to her mouth. "Excuse me?"

"You heard me."

"But…but you can't do that," she sputtered.

"Watch me."

Dear heavens, he was serious. She could see it in the hard glitter of his eyes and intractable set of his jaw. She'd never seen him look tougher or more formidable, cloaked with a dark, dangerous edge. She would have panicked if she hadn't also seen something else. Something that actually gave her hope.

There in the tawny gold of his eyes, she caught the unmistakable flame of desire. He might fight it, he might deny it, he might have attempted to bury it beneath endless layers of ice, but she didn't doubt for a minute he felt it.

Daisy decided to test the possibility. "What am I supposed to do while you're keeping me here?" She caught it again, just the merest flash. But it answered her question without his having to say a word. "You can't be serious."

"You chose to come here. By doing so you assume the risk and consequences of your actions."

She invaded his personal space until they were only inches apart. Not that he backed down. "And making love is the risk and consequence I assumed by showing up on your doorstep? Oh, excuse me. According to you we've never made love, have we?" She wrapped air quotes around the words, "made love." "I seem to recall your telling me it was just sex."

A cool smile snagged the corners of his mouth. "According to *you,* amazing sex."

Her temper shot straight through the roof. "Oh! How dare you throw that in my face after all this time. And how dare you decide to keep me here against my will. Just because you haven't gotten any in a while and I conveniently appear on your doorstep, you think you can toss me in your bed and have your wicked way with me?"

"Yes."

Her mouth opened and closed, but she couldn't seem to do more than make odd little choking noises. Finally, her vocal cords kicked in. "Yes? That's all you have to say? *Yes?* Have you lost your mind?"

He went nose-to-nose with her. "Once again, yes! I lost my mind nineteen months, fifteen days, six hours, twenty-eight minutes and twelve seconds ago. And I want it back, which is precisely what you're going to do. Having you here in my bed should return some modicum of sanity to me. It's a perfectly logical solution to an utterly illogical problem."

Daisy couldn't recall Justice ever coming so close to losing his temper. Not to this extent. Always in the past he'd shown impressive self-control and restraint. Whereas she'd fly off in a thousand different directions, spewing emotional lava like a human volcano, he would pull tighter, deeper, one by one shutting off all those hot, torrid outlets until he had everything tamped down and safely buried.

Well, not this time. Not now. She knew that if she pushed so much as one more button, she could stand back and watch him blow. Her finger itched to try it, and yet, she hesitated. What would be the cost if she tipped him over the edge? What would it do to him to have that control ripped away? He'd hate it. Despise himself. And she simply couldn't do that to him. If he ever opened to her, actually expressed those emotions and revealed his vulnerability, it would be his choice. She wouldn't force it on him.

Daisy allowed the seconds to slip by, allowed the simmer and boil to cool. Allowed the volcano to slip back into dormancy. "You have a lot of nerve, Justice," she told him quietly.

"You're correct." He wrapped control around himself like a blanket of snow. Even so, she could sense the heat of desire lingering beneath the ice. "That doesn't change the fact that you'll do whatever I tell you."

For some reason his comment made her smile. "Anything?"

"Anything and everything," he confirmed.

Her amusement faded and she lowered her gaze so she wouldn't betray her reaction. She doubted she could conceal the intense longing that gripped her. The underpinning of desperation and want. It wasn't fair. Not after what he'd done. Not after all the time and distance separating them. "I thought you didn't want me."

To her relief, Justice didn't deny it. "Apparently, I was wrong. I guess we both were."

"An affair, is that what you're proposing?" She looked at him again, allowing a hint of her own yearning to slip through. "I stay here for however long it takes you to find a new place to hide—"

"I'm not hiding."

Daisy couldn't help herself. She laughed, the sound almost painful. "Oh, please."

"I'm protecting my privacy. If the general public knew where I lived—"

"The general public couldn't care less. Maybe the media would express some interest. But I suspect the only ones you need to worry about are other mad scientist wannabes." She leaned her hip against the kitchen table. "So, what's the real reason, Justice?"

He took a slow drink of his water, no doubt to give himself time to consider the most logical response to her question. He must have come up empty, because he asked instead, "How did you find me?"

She'd been waiting for that, wondering when he'd get around to it. "I had help, which is another reason you can't keep me here against my will. Jett will eventually grow concerned and alert the authorities."

"Jett." His eyes flamed before he regained control. "Boyfriend? Husband? Lover?"

Two could play this game. She folded her arms across her chest and lifted an eyebrow. And waited.

"How did this Jett person find us, Pretorius?" Justice asked while his heated gaze remained locked with hers.

To Daisy's shock, a disembodied voice responded. "I'm working on it."

"Work harder. I want him traced and shut down."

"You think I don't know that? I know that. This Jett is good. Real good."

"I thought you were the best."

"Go to hell, Justice."

Much to Daisy's relief, a peeved tone rippled through Pretorius's voice, confirming his status as a living, breathing human versus a machine. Even though Justice had claimed Pretorius was his uncle, she wouldn't have put it past him to have considered that some sort of private joke. Of course, that would mean Justice would need to possess a sense of humor, something he'd probably worked long and hard to eradicate, along with every other emotion.

Well, except desire. That remained fully operational.

"I think I found how he traced us. Shutting him down. Okay, he's cut off."

Justice offered a wintry smile that perfectly matched the raw November day. "Is that it?" she asked. "We're now invisible to Jett? You do realize that I got here with a GPS. I was tracked every step of the way."

"It won't take long to relocate."

"I find that difficult to believe unless you already have a backup site ready to go." The glitter in his tawny gaze confirmed her guess. "Okay, fine. You know something, Justice? You go right ahead. Keep me here until you and your uncle are ready to run to wherever your new cave is located. Then you can hang from the rafters in the privacy of your latest den of doom and gloom. Frankly, I don't give a damn."

"I already told you we're not in hiding. And mad scientists hide in basements not in rafters."

Okay, that was definitely a joke. Who knew? Not that it mattered. She brushed the comment aside with a sweep of her hand. "Whatever. That's not why I'm here. You're so worried about the hows and whys of my finding you that you've totally ignored the main question."

"Such as the reason you wrote twenty-six letters and requested they be forwarded to me? Not to mention why, after all this time, you've gone to so much trouble to track me down? Those main questions?"

He'd received her letters and *still* never got in touch? Fury ripped through her. "Yes, those main questions," she said through gritted teeth.

"Don't keep me in suspense. What could you possibly have to say that we didn't cover nineteen months and fifteen days ago?"

He wanted it straight? Fine. She'd give it to him straight. "You have a daughter."

Five

Justice had always considered himself a rational man. Intelligent. Sensible. Calm and collected. His emotions firmly within his control. But with those four simple words he discovered just how mistaken he could be. Only one other time had he experienced this severe a brain disconnect—the hours following his accident. He opened his mouth to say something, only to discover that every last word had emptied from his mind.

"Wha—"

"What's her name? It's Noelle."

"Whe—"

"When was she born? Eleven months and a handful of days ago. Christmas morning, to be exact. If you need further exactitude, which I'm sure you do, they recorded the precise time on her birth certificate. I'll arrange for you to receive a copy."

"Ho—"

"How do I know you're the father? Because you're the

only man I've slept with in the past three years. No doubt you'll want a DNA test and I have no objection. I thought you should know about Noelle, so I've spent the past year and a half trying to track you down without success. But then, since you received all my letters, you already know that, don't you?" She paused for a beat. "Are you listening, Pretorius?"

"Uh—" came his uncle's disembodied voice.

"I thought so. I can hear the family resemblance. It only took Jett a few short weeks to find you." She shot Justice a steely look. "I think that means my computer expert outcomputes your computer expert. Now. What were you saying about keeping me here?"

The logjam clogging Justice's vocal cords cleared. "Son of a *bitch!*"

Daisy planted her hands on her hips, glorious in her outrage. "I trust you won't use that sort of language around our daughter. She's quite verbal for so young an age. She tries to parrot everything you say."

"I want her."

Something very much like hurt flashed across Daisy's expression and her eyes darkened to the deep green of a mountain forest. For some reason it shredded his defenses and arrowed straight to the emotional core of him. How was that possible? How could a single look possess the power to stir a combination of guilt and defensiveness? He'd worked diligently for over a year and half to eradicate any and all reactions to her from his emotional makeup. And yet from the instant she appeared on his doorstep he'd discovered that he hadn't eradicated anything at all. One glimpse of her elegant face glaring up at the camera and desire came storming back, eclipsing logic and self-determination.

It defied comprehension.

He hastened to amend his earlier statement. "I want both of you."

He hadn't helped his cause. Her chin shot up and her eyes

flashed with green fire, full of feminine fury, mingled with a gut-wrenching anguish. "I don't think you deserve me. And I know you don't deserve Noelle."

"If that's what you believe, why are you here?"

He caught her wariness before she wiped every thought and emotion from her face, closing down and shutting him out. She'd never done that before. He suspected she'd never been capable of it until recently. When they'd last been together she'd been open and forthcoming, her opinions and feelings out there for everyone to see. Was he responsible for so dramatic a change? Had their night together caused her to regard the world with such caution? He flinched from the thought, from the idea he was capable of inflicting that level of pain on anyone, though for reasons he couldn't bring himself to analyze, Daisy in particular.

"You deserved to know about your daughter. Now that you do, I'm finished here."

She was keeping something from him, he could tell. "It's more than that, isn't it?" He could also tell she had zero intention of explaining herself. "Never mind. Considering how guarded I am about my own privacy, I won't intrude on yours."

"Thank you."

"But if I can help, I will." He had no idea where the words came from. He certainly hadn't planned to say them, an unfathomable lapse on his part, but they caught her attention.

She studied his face for a long, tense moment. Then her head jerked in a nod. "Thanks. I appreciate it."

Whether she realized it or not, Daisy's announcement offered him the perfect opportunity to achieve the goals he'd set more than two years ago—to create a family. To have someone in his life who mattered. Who cared. Though she didn't and couldn't meet his conditions for an engineering apprentice, any more than those for the perfect wife, the potential existed to shape her to fit many of the same param-

eters. Hell, he'd even be willing to alter his lifestyle somewhat to suit her requirements for a husband. Within reason,
of course.

And then there was Noelle. He struggled to draw air into
his lungs at the thought of his progeny. *A daughter.* He had
a child! It stunned him how much that simple fact changed
the means by which he processed information. He found he
craved her, sight unseen. Wanted and needed them both in
ways he found inexplicable. No matter what it took, he'd give
Daisy whatever she required in order to have his ready-made
family part of his life.

He crossed to a sturdy wooden table and pulled out a chair,
formulating a swift game plan. "Let's sit and talk about this.
Are you hungry?"

Annoyance flashed. "Let me get this straight. Now that
you know about Noelle you're willing to feed me?"

"No," he responded mildly. "Since I planned to keep you
here until we relocated, I would have gotten around to feeding
you. Eventually."

That provoked a smile. A tiny one, but a smile nonetheless.
The impact of it far exceeded what it should have, based on
all rational consideration. And yet, just as at the engineering
conference, it drew him in, put thoughts and ideas in his
head he'd spent every day since their night together working
to eradicate. How many potential apprentice/wives had he
interviewed since Daisy? How many times had Pretorius
tweaked his Pretorius Program in an effort to find the
"perfect" woman? How many failures had there been?

And all because none of them were Daisy, he now realized.

Oh, they'd suited his conditions to a T. Every last miserable one of them had engineering credentials. Were brilliant, rational, sensible women in complete control of their
emotions. A few were even more attractive than Daisy, though
for some inexplicable reason their beauty left him cold. To
be fair, none of them revealed any true meanness that he'd

noticed, still he wouldn't call them kind. Perhaps their very lack of emotional depth prevented them from exhibiting the qualities Daisy possessed in distressing excess.

Regardless, his search had ultimately resulted in only one serious candidate…along with the indelible memory of Daisy. Now he had the ideal opportunity to mold the woman he actually wanted into the perfect wife.

"I thought we were going to talk," she prompted with another of her irresistible smiles.

"Talking is the easy part."

Again, the wariness. "And the not-so easy part?" she asked.

"I don't cook and neither does Pretorius."

She glanced around. "Maybe that explains the lack of appliances."

"There's a fully stocked refrigerator and freezer in the cabinet behind me, as well as a full complement of appliances." He took a seat beside her. "I also have someone stop in once a day and prepare our meals, so you can cross that concern off your list."

She blinked. "I didn't realize I had a list."

"I'm making one for you."

Daisy's eyes narrowed. "And why would you do that? And why should it matter whether or not you can cook, or whether or not you have someone fixing your meals? It has nothing to do with me."

Now for the hard part. No point in delaying the inevitable. Better to get right to it. "It's about to have a lot to do with you, because I want you and Noelle to move in here with me and I'll do whatever it takes to make that happen."

She shook her head before he even finished speaking. "Forget it, Justice. I'm not interested in having you in my life any more than you're interested in being in mine."

He lifted an eyebrow. "You'd rather share custody of Noelle?"

The breath left Daisy's lungs in a rush. "What?"

"You said she's mine. Now that I know about her existence, I'm willing and able to be a father to her. There's only two ways that'll work. Either we live together or we shuttle her back and forth between us. I'm thinking it's in our daughter's best interest for her to live with both of us. Together."

Her gaze swept the room and he struggled to see it through her eyes. Despite the state-of-the-art equipment and electronics tucked neatly behind warm oak cabinets, it came up lacking. Empty. Cold. Aw, hell. Dark and dusty, even with the lights.

"You want us to live out here, in the middle of nowhere?" she asked in disbelief. "What sort of life is that for a child?"

"We can work around any of your objections," he insisted doggedly. "There are reasons I choose to live in the middle of nowhere."

"Such as?"

"Pretorius? Permission, please."

There was a momentary silence, then, "Tell her."

"My uncle has a social anxiety disorder. It's one of the reasons I was put in foster care after the death of my parents. The courts didn't consider Pretorius an acceptable guardian."

Compassion swept across Daisy's expression and he realized that it was an innate part of her character. It always had been. "Agoraphobia?" She hazarded a guess.

"That's probably part of it. More, it's people in general he has difficulty handling."

"Huh. I have that same problem…with certain people."

He acknowledged the hit with a cool smile. "Whereas he needs the isolation, I value my privacy. When I turned eighteen and had nowhere to go, my uncle opened his home to me, even though he found it a very difficult adjustment. Since then, it's worked for us. Or rather, it did."

"Should I assume something changed?"

Time to be honest with her. Totally honest. "Yes. It changed a couple of years ago."

"What happened a couple of years—" He caught her dawning comprehension and again that deep flash of compassion. How did she do it? How did she open herself up like that and let everyone in? Especially when it guaranteed she would be hurt in the process. "Oh, Justice. The car wreck?"

He nodded. "It made me realize what I had wasn't enough."

"And…?"

He chose his words with care. It felt like tiptoeing through a minefield. "I asked Pretorius to rewrite a business program he marketed a few years ago. I gave him a set of parameters combining qualities important to me, with characteristics that would also be compatible with my uncle."

She stared blankly. "You just lost me."

"He asked me to find him a wife," Pretorius interrupted. "One that we'd both like."

Justice swore. "I'm telling this story, old man."

"And I'm just filling in the parts you seem to be skipping over."

"I was getting to them. I just wanted to do this in a logical order."

Pretorius snorted. "Right. And E-equals-MC-you're-full-of-crap."

Damn it to hell. "Computer, close circuit to kitchen and keep it closed until I say otherwise."

"No, I want to hear—" Pretorius's voice was cut off midsentence.

Justice took a deep, steadying breath. "Now, where was I?"

He could see the laughter in Daisy's eyes before gold-tipped lashes swept downward, concealing her expression. "I believe you were explaining how you used a computer program to find a wife." The merest hint of amusement threaded through her words.

"It made perfect sense at the time."

"Of course it did."

"The Pretorius Program has been quite successful at choosing the perfect employee in the business sector." He heard the defensive edge slashing through his comment and took a moment to gather himself. What was it about Daisy that caused him to lose his composure with such ease and frequency? "I had more specific requirements to take into consideration for a wife, so Pretorius tweaked the parameters."

"What sort of specific requirements and what parameters?"

Hell, no. He would not walk down that road. "That's not important."

Unfortunately, she seemed unusually adept at adding two and two together, squaring it and leaping to a completely illogical, though accurate, conclusion. "You were looking for a wife at that engineering conference, weren't you? That's why you were so mad when you discovered I wasn't an engineer."

"That's a distinct possibility," he admitted.

She leaned forward, staring intently, her spring-green eyes disturbing in the extreme. "Are you telling me that Pretorius devised a computer program to find you the perfect woman and she was supposed to be at that conference?"

Damn, damn, damn. "Yes."

"Are you seriously going to sit there and admit that you thought you could waltz into that conference, check out the women your uncle's program selected and convince one of them to marry you?"

He gritted his teeth. "Engineers are very logical. The women involved would have seen that we were an excellent match."

Her mouth dropped open. "And agreed to marry you right then and there?"

"That would have been helpful, though unlikely."

"You *think?*"

He suspected from her tone that the question was both rhetorical and a bit sarcastic. Just in case he was mistaken, he gave her a straight answer. "Yes. But Pretorius suggested a way around that."

"Oh, this I have to hear."

"He suggested I offer her a position as my apprentice. That would allow us an opportunity to get to know each other better before committing to marriage. It would also allow me to determine whether she was acceptable to Pretorius."

"Huh." Daisy mulled that over. "Okay, that's not such a bad plan. So explain something to me. It's been almost two years. Why don't you have an apprentice/wife by now?"

He would have given anything to avoid this conversation. But he suspected that unless he put all his cards on the table, he'd lose any chance at having a family. A real family. And over the past two years he'd discovered he wanted that more than anything else. Needed the connection before the ice crystallizing in his veins won and he lost all ability to feel. "It would seem the computer program contained a flaw."

"Remarkable."

"Agreed." He frowned. "In retrospect, I realize that there are some indefinable qualities that prove difficult to adapt to a computer program."

"Wow. Who would have thought. Enlighten me. What sort of indefinable qualities are we talking about?"

Justice had given it a lot of thought over the ensuing months and as irrational and unscientific as it was, there'd been only one inescapable conclusion. "I believe it must have been chemical in nature and therefore extremely difficult to quantify."

"In English, please?"

He stood and crossed the room to give himself some breathing space. "I didn't want them. I wanted you." The words hung in the air, frank and inescapable. And completely, painfully honest. "It's not logical. I can't explain it. It just is."

She shook her head and to his alarm he saw tears gleam in her too-expressive eyes. "Don't, Justice. I can't go there again. Not when I know how you really feel about me. That you still hold me responsible for losing your scholarship and being sent to some hideous foster home."

He leaned his hip against the counter and folded his arms across his chest. "The truth?"

She forced out a watery smile. "Will it hurt?"

He weighed the possibility. "I don't believe so."

"In that case, I guess I can handle it."

"Six months, three days, twenty-two hours and nine minutes ago I came to a conclusion."

"And what conclusion is that?"

"That even if I'd known before we made love that I'd lose my scholarship, I'm not positive I could have resisted. I would have tried due to your age, but to be perfectly frank, at seventeen I lacked the maturity to make decisions based on intellect rather than hormonal imperative."

Her smile wobbled, grew. "Does that mean you forgive me?"

"It wouldn't be rational to continue to hold a grudge." He frowned, picking through his words. "Though I no longer feel any anger in association with what occurred, I still possess a certain level of resentment. But considering that my success in the field of robotics hasn't been negatively impacted by those events, even resentment is an unreasonable response."

"Yes, it is," she agreed.

"I also never asked whether our relationship had a negative impact on your life," he found himself saying, much to his surprise. "Were you negatively impacted?"

"Yes."

He frowned in concern. "How?" A sudden thought struck and he froze. "You didn't get pregnant, did you?"

"No, nothing like that. I was hurt because you left without a word. Of course, now I understand why. But at the time it broke my heart." Her chin quivered ever so slightly. "I missed you so much."

An odd feeling raced through him, a yearning combined with an almost forgotten pain. "I missed you, too," he confessed. "I didn't want to, since I blamed you for what happened. But you were the first real friend I'd ever had."

"Oh, Justice."

She escaped her chair and threw herself into his arms. At the first touch of her soft form colliding against his hard angles, he discovered he'd made a serious miscalculation. Whatever they'd experienced all those months ago hadn't dissipated over time as he'd anticipated. If anything, the craving had grown progressively worse. It might not be logical, but it was unquestionably true. He took the only action he deemed reasonable.

He kissed her.

Alice down the rabbit hole.

Only in this case Daisy tumbled head over heels down the hole and landed in a crazy, new world. Or maybe it wasn't all that new. She'd worked so hard to forget what it had been like to lose herself in his arms. To know his kiss and have it sweep her away. To reach for something she thought long lost to her. He took his time reminding her of every moment of those lost memories.

Pleasure erupted, a tidal wave of sparkling joy, rushing through her without rhyme or reason. Not that it was love. She couldn't love him. Refused to allow it. Passion. Lust. Sexual attraction. All those things she could accept, but not love. And she'd do everything within her power to avoid feeling an emotional attachment to a man who spent a lifetime suppressing them. She couldn't deal with the despair and disillusionment again. It was too painful.

His mouth shifted across hers, deepening the kiss—a kiss that shouldn't have improved since the last time they were together, but somehow had. She didn't know whether it came from a growing familiarity or nearly two months of longing. She could only acknowledge the truth of it before going under, drowning beneath the cascade of sensations swamping her.

How did he do it? How did he stir such a helpless reaction? Her lips parted beneath his delicious invasion, opening to the heat. He was a man of logic and control, and yet she felt the instant that control slipped and shattered. He demanded, then tempted. Teased, then seduced. He touched her, kissed her, shifted his body against hers in a rhythm they'd both perfected that long-ago night. And yet, it might have been yesterday, the movements as familiar to her as they were arousing, and she found herself surrendering to the raw power of that primal song that played whenever they came together.

His hands cupped her face, tilting her head so he could more fully explore her mouth. She lost herself in the kiss while the sweetest of memories slid over and through her. Memories of their last night together when he'd taken her countless times, the final one sweet and tender beyond bearing. She suspected it had been then that she'd conceived Noelle, then that passion had caused them to forget a bedside table drawer full of caution. Then that he'd forever branded himself on her, heart and body and soul.

No! Oh, no, no, no. How could she be so foolish?

Daisy ripped free of his embrace and put the width of the table between them. She'd come here, dead certain in her ability to hold Justice at arm's length, and instead all he'd had to do was touch her and she tumbled into his arms and surrendered. Did she think that everything that had gone so dramatically wrong twenty endless months ago, a single kiss could set right?

Swearing silently, she snatched up her bottle of water and hastily unscrewed the lid and took a long swallow while she struggled to gather her thoughts. "When you said you wanted me and Noelle to move in and you'll do whatever it takes to make that happen—"

"I have always found that positive reinforcement works best."

"You'd bribe me to live with you, Justice?" She took her time recapping the bottle. "Or perhaps that kiss was part of your positive reinforcement."

"Only if it worked. Otherwise, what can I offer that will convince you to do as I request?"

"Do you realize that you sound like a computer whenever you get tense?" Based on the blank look he gave her, he didn't. "Bribery won't work, Justice. Nor will kissing me."

"What will?"

She stood and crossed the kitchen to the shuttered window. "Is there any way to open this?"

"Computer, open window at Kitchen, Station 1A."

A soft hum sounded and the shutters parted. This side of the house faced a long, rolling valley that must be stunning in the spring. Right now, with winter on the verge of overtaking them, it offered a raw, unforgiving beauty. Without the green of spring to cloak it, or flowers to add bright color and texture, only the bare bones remained. Nature at its most stark, without the pretty artifice to soften the harsh truth.

And the harsh truth was that she hadn't been completely honest with Justice about why she'd tracked him down. Their daughter, Noelle, had been a huge part of it—the main part. But there was another reason, one she kept from him, one she found difficult to admit, even to herself. Ever since their night together she'd been unable to paint. She'd attempted countless times, without success. But, whatever creative spark, whatever gift or talent she'd been given, had evaporated as though it never existed. It had driven her to extreme measures, to allowing Jett to use every means at her disposal to find Justice's hideaway in the hope that she could set right something that had gone hideously wrong—both for Noelle's sake, as well as her own.

He'd asked her to stay and she wanted to, wanted with all her heart to be with him and discover if they couldn't recapture some part of what they'd shared once upon a time. Why was she hesitating, when he offered to give her just that?

Because he wasn't offering her love.

Well, too bad. She could move in and take her chances, or she could share custody of Noelle. She released her breath in a sigh and turned to face him. "No bribery, Justice. And I can't commit to staying with you permanently. But I am willing to come for a visit as your guest. We'll try it out for a few months and see how it goes. Sort of like what you intended with your apprentice/wife program. Will that do?"

"For now." His gaze strayed to the window. "I wouldn't wait too long, though. Winter's coming."

"It shouldn't take longer than a week to organize. Is there enough room for all of us?"

"This place has a dozen bedrooms. I'll get them ready and you can pick whichever ones you want."

"And Pretorius? How will he handle having visitors?"

Justice frowned. "He has his own section of the house. So long as you don't intrude, he should be fine."

Daisy nodded. "Then I'll see you in a week." She turned and started from the kitchen, pausing at the last minute. And that's when she accepted the heartrending truth. "Our lives will never be the same again. Everything changed twenty months ago, and there's no going back now, is there? Not for either of us."

And without a backward look, she fled.

Justice stood unmoving while the house settled into

silence, returning to its cold air of detachment. Always a house, never a home. Always cold, never filled with light and laughter and warmth.

"You're right. There's no going back," he whispered. "But what you don't realize is…I don't want to go back. I can't live like that anymore."

Daisy gritted her teeth, zigging to avoid driving through yet another pothole, this one the size of a large crater. If she ended up staying with Justice for any length of time, she and Justice were going to have words about this road.

"Almost there." Excitement ricocheted through Jett's voice, making her sound far younger than sixteen. "Just another one-point-four miles and we should be able to see it."

"See it?" Noelle parroted. Only it came out more like "feet?"

Dear heavens, if it wasn't Dora the GPS keeping track of every inch of every mile, it was Jett. And Daisy was willing to bet her last tube of Old Holland Viridian Green oil paint that when Noelle was a few years older she'd be every bit as bad.

"We're surrounded," she muttered to Aggie, her house-keeper. "Better get used to it now. There's worse and you're about to meet him."

"I can handle it," came the calm, seasoned response.

Years ago Aggie had been an elementary school teacher. She'd taken early retirement in order to nurse her husband through a lengthy illness, only to discover their savings exhausted by the time he died. The realization that she had no choice but to return to work coincided with Noelle's birth and Daisy's decision that she needed help with cooking and general housekeeping chores, especially after she'd assumed guardianship of Jett. She'd hired Aggie on the spot. To their mutual delight, the four of them had cemented into a cozy little family, one Justice would have to accept—if he wanted them to remain in Colorado.

"Are you sure Mr. St. John won't mind that you brought all of us along?" Aggie asked with a hint of nervousness.

Daisy started to say she didn't give a hot damn whether Mr. St. John minded, but aware of a backseat full of big ears, she modified her reply. "The four of us are a family. That means we're a package deal. Don't worry. Justice will be cool with it."

A tiny sigh of relief issued from behind her, making Daisy aware that Jett was also feeling apprehensive. She always appeared so self-assured, it came as a bit of a shock the few times she reverted to the nervous, suspicious girl she'd been when Daisy's parents had first taken her in as a foster child.

"I can't believe I'm about to meet the man behind Sinjin," Jett said.

"Finfin?"

"That's your daddy, Red."

"Daddy."

That word came out clear as a bell. For some reason it caused Daisy to flinch and Aggie shot her a sympathetic look. "I'm sure he'll make a wonderful father."

"There's no question Noelle needs him." Her own inadequacies threatened to overwhelm her. "Lord knows, I can't meet all of her needs."

"No parent can give their child everything they require. It's not possible," Aggie was quick to reassure. "If you're very lucky, you can cover most of it between the two of you and hope that friends and family and teachers cover the rest. Just loving them goes a long way."

But was Justice capable of love? Was it programmed into his software or had that particular upgrade been wiped from his hard drive? Only time would tell. At long last the car crested the final hill and they coasted down to the sprawling homestead. She parked near the steps leading to the main house and cut the engine.

"Okay, everyone grab something and let's get inside." Together they tromped up the steps. She gave the door a tentative shove, relieved when it opened to her touch. At least she wouldn't have to threaten her way in like last time. That would have been a tad embarrassing. "See?" she said with a reassuring smile. "Let's head for the kitchen and get something to drink while we wait for Justice."

It didn't take long. Within a minute he stepped into the kitchen, his tawny gaze sweeping the group. One look warned Daisy he hadn't taken the unexpected guests well. He reminded her of the panther she'd immortalized in her storybooks, stalking into the room, looking sleek and predatory and incredibly dangerous. For a man so proud of his restraint and emotional detachment, he certainly gave a fine imitation of someone who'd gotten his tail in a twist.

For a long, almost painful moment, his gaze lingered on his daughter. Tears pricked Daisy's eyes at the intense longing that ripped apart his expression. It tarnished his eyes and crept deep into the crevices bracketing his mouth. Then his lashes dipped downward, concealing his expression, and he deliberately turned away. She suspected he didn't have a choice, not if he hoped to maintain even a modicum of self-control.

"You said a week," he all but growled. "It's been ten days, three hours and fourteen minutes."

"Sorry about that. It took longer than I expected to get everyone organized. I did email you about the change in dates." He swept the assembled group with a look that probably would have decimated everyone on the spot if Daisy hadn't stepped between Justice and her family to intercept the full blast of it. "Problem?" she asked sweetly.

"A moment of your time?"

His voice had lowered to a threatening rumble, forcing

Daisy to spare her family a reassuring smile. "If you'd wait here," she requested, easing Noelle into Aggie's arms. "There are drinks in the refrigerator, assuming you can figure out where it's hidden."

"I'm on it," Jett announced brightly, her gaze practically eating Justice alive.

"Behave," Daisy mouthed to the teen. Though why she bothered, she couldn't say. She might as well tell a mouse to stay away from the cheese.

Not giving Daisy a chance to issue any further instructions, Justice snagged her arm and drew her from the room. They retraced the path to the front door and continued on in the opposite direction to a large office with a spectacular view of the Rockies. She didn't think he used this room any more often than any of the others on this level. The same feeling of neglect hung over the few furnishings it contained. But at least the shutters were open.

The early afternoon burned across the mountains, coating them in every shade from deep royal blue to the dense purple of eggplant. Trees, bare and stark, slept beside stands of conifers, the green rich with the promise that life would one day return to the windswept landscape. In the distance snowcapped peaks shoved upward against a remote sky, the pale blue expanse winter-hard and slashed with high streaks of gray cirrus clouds. It made her itch to grab her sketchbook and pencils and have at it. But ever since she'd lost her creative spark, she'd been afraid to do even that much, afraid she'd be forced to concede, once and for all, that she'd lost all artistic ability.

Releasing a sigh, Daisy turned from the view and discovered Justice pacing the room in perfect imitation of a sleek jungle cat. Or, to be precise, an infuriated jungle cat ready to attack at the least provocation. He also held the odd spherical device he'd played with the night Noelle had been conceived, twisting and turning it into shape after shape.

"All right," Justice announced, bringing her to earth with a thud. "Let's hear it."

"What do you want to hear?" she asked. As if she didn't know.

He regarded her with burning, narrowed eyes. "You know damn well, Daisy. Who the hell are all those people?"

Six

"One of 'those people' was your daughter," Daisy retorted calmly. "And if you'd given me a moment to introduce the others, you'd know who the hell they are."

Anger flared and the sleek sphere stuttered in Justice's hands. "Damn it, woman!"

Did he just call her "woman"? She approached, her anger rising to meet his. "Now that I'm here, I think it's time to discuss my conditions for staying."

That stopped him dead in his tracks. "Conditions? You never mentioned conditions to me."

"Well, now I am." She didn't give him time to debate the issue. "Condition One. If you want us here for longer than the next five minutes, you're going to have to adjust your language. Noelle is unbelievably verbal and tries to repeat just about everything she hears. I won't have her swearing before she even turns one."

"Hel—" He broke off and then swore again. "Fair enough. I'll do my best. I can't promise I'll be perfect."

"Condition Two. My name is Daisy. Call me 'woman' in that tone of voice or swear at me again, and I'm out the door. And so is your daughter. Got it?"

He clenched his teeth together so tightly it was a wonder they didn't crack. Even so, he conceded the point with an abrupt nod. "Any other conditions?"

She simply smiled. "Third, Aggie and Jett are members of my household, and where I go, they go."

He must have picked up on her determination. She could practically see him adjusting his mental paradigm or thought processes or whatever the heck went on inside that amazing brain of his. "Who is Aggie?" he asked, the question so prosaic Daisy almost laughed.

"Aggie's a former elementary school teacher and currently my cook and housekeeper. Since I'm a disaster in the kitchen and since the four of us need to eat, I hired her to take care of all things domestic."

He perked up a little over that. "She cooks?"

"And cleans," Daisy stressed. She eyed the room in open displeasure. "Seriously, Justice, this place is a disaster. I can't believe you're comfortable living like this."

He glanced around, though she suspected he didn't see the office and surrounding rooms the same way she did. "It's just a bit of dust, and I don't live in this section of the house."

It didn't take much thought to figure out where he did live. "Mad scientist plus secret location equals mysterious, hidden lab?"

"Something like that," he conceded.

"A spotless mysterious, hidden lab?"

"Of course."

"Well, since you now have guests who will be living in this section of the house, we'll need our accommodations to be as spotless as your lab."

He examined the room again, this time really looking—this time finally seeing. She could tell from his gathering frown that until that moment he'd been oblivious to the full extent of the problem. "I've been focused on a project and didn't realize how bad…" He blew out a sigh. "I apologize. I should have done more to prepare for your arrival."

"We'll handle it."

The "we" succeeded in returning his attention to his unexpected guests. "You've explained Aggie. Who's the scary Goth girl?" he asked.

Daisy couldn't help but smile. "That's Jett."

"Jett." He froze. "Not *that* Jett. Not your computer expert."

"That's the one," she took delight in confirming. "She was my parents' foster child. After Dad suffered a heart attack, it became clear she'd have to move to a new home. Jett decided she didn't want to start over somewhere else and asked me to become her foster parent instead."

"This is November. Shouldn't she be in school?"

"She received her GED at sixteen. She's currently considering colleges."

Justice's brows shot upward. "How old is she? She looks about twelve."

"She'll turn seventeen in a few months. Jett can give you the days, hours and minutes, right down to the seconds if you want a more exact number."

"She's smart."

"Scary smart. Like you, scary smart." Daisy hesitated. "Like Noelle."

His gaze sharpened. It didn't take him long to process her comment and come up with the correct explanation. "That's why you're here."

"One of the reasons, yes." No point in going into any of the others. Those would become apparent over time. "It's clear she requires someone who's going to understand the way she thinks. Right now she has Jett, which is a huge help. But, Jett won't be around forever. Plus, there's no male figure in

Noelle's life other than my father and now that he has health issues..."

At the mention of her parents, his expression closed over, turning as cold and bleak as the mountains at his back. "I don't want them anywhere near Noelle. Not after what they did to me."

Daisy stared in disbelief. "You can't keep them out of her life."

"Watch me."

"Condition Five."

"Four."

"Whatever. My parents are part of my life, the same way Jett and Aggie are. Deal with it."

A muscle jerked in his jaw and his eyes burned like liquid gold. "Any other conditions?" He bit off each word as though they scorched his tongue.

"You haven't agreed to my last one."

"Why don't we leave that one open for future discussion."

She refused to allow it. "Why don't we put that one to rest right now, because if you think for one little minute I'm going to deny my parents access to their only grandchild, you can think again." She held up her hand. "And before you decide to break Condition One again—"

"Too damn late!"

"I suggest you put yourself in my place. In Noelle's place. You're the one who walked away, Justice." She struggled to conceal her hurt with limited success. "My parents have been with me every step of the way. You haven't."

"Only because I didn't know."

"You're a brilliant man. You should have considered that possibility and made sure. At the very least, you should have contacted me after the first dozen letters." Could he hear the pain bleeding through her words? "Instead, you went out of your way to make certain I couldn't find you again. That we'd never see each other again."

Play the Lucky Hearts Game

and get...

2 FREE BOOKS and
2 FREE MYSTERY GIFTS...
YOURS TO KEEP!

Yes! I have scratched off the gold card.
Please send me my *2 FREE BOOKS* and
2 FREE MYSTERY GIFTS (gifts are worth about $10).
I understand that I am under no obligation to purchase
any books as explained on the back of this card.

Scratch Here!
Then look below to see what your
cards get you...2 Free Books
& 2 Free Mystery Gifts!

225/326 HDL FJDQ

FIRST NAME

LAST NAME

ADDRESS

APT.#

CITY

STATE/PROV.   ZIP/POSTAL CODE

Visit us online at
www.ReaderService.com

Twenty-one gets you
2 FREE BOOKS and
2 FREE MYSTERY GIFTS!

Twenty gets you
2 FREE BOOKS!

Nineteen gets you
1 FREE BOOK!

TRY AGAIN!

Offer limited to one per household and not applicable to series that subscriber is currently receiving.

Your Privacy—The Reader Service is committed to protecting your privacy. Our Privacy Policy is available online at www.ReaderService.com or upon request from the Reader Service. We make a portion of our mailing list available to reputable third parties that offer products we believe may interest you. If you prefer that we not exchange your name with third parties, or if you wish to clarify or modify your communication preferences, please visit us at www.ReaderService.com/consumerschoice or write to us at Reader Service Preference Service, P.O. Box 9062, Buffalo, NY 14269. Include your complete name and address.

© 2011 HARLEQUIN ENTERPRISES LIMITED. Printed in the U.S.A.

▼ **DETACH AND MAIL CARD TODAY!** ▼

H-D-11/11

"That's not true. I would have—" He broke off and swung around to face the picture window. "Any other conditions?"

"Do you agree to my last one?"

"Yes."

He sounded so bleak it almost unnerved her. She took a moment to gather her thoughts before pressing forward. "Condition Ten."

"Five."

"I'm holding the others in reserve." She didn't give him time to argue the point. "I need a room for a studio. One with windows." She had no idea whether she'd actually use the studio. She considered it more of a last-ditch effort. Because deep inside she secretly wondered whether she'd ever paint again. And the thought flat-out terrified her. "Unshuttered windows, if you don't mind."

He shrugged. "You can take a look around and see if anything suits. Make sure it's on this level or upstairs. The basement is off-limits to everyone."

"Is that where your uncle lives?"

"Yes. It's also where my lab is located."

Justice faced her once again. The sphere flowed through his fingers, assuming one shape after another. First a cylinder, then a pyramid, then something that twisted in on itself, making her dizzy. "What is that thing?" she asked.

"I call it Rumi. It helps me think." He'd regained his self-control and regarded her with a calm, icy expression that seemed to lower the temperature in the room by several degrees. She shivered, waiting for snowflakes to start drifting from the ceiling. "My turn," he announced.

Uh-oh. She hadn't anticipated this and should have. "You have conditions?"

"You thought you'd be the only one?"

She retreated a pace, even knowing it portrayed a certain defensiveness. "Okay, fine. What are your conditions?"

He took a step in her direction, following in the path of

her retreat, all the while the sphere twisted, twisted, twisted. "One. It is your responsibility to keep everyone out of the basement. That includes you. Having you and Noelle here is tough enough for Pretorius. The addition of two more people will be extremely difficult for him. He needs to know that he's safe in his area of the house. Am I clear on this point?"

"Crystal."

"Two." Another step closer. "I have a routine. Disruptions to that routine are unacceptable."

He couldn't be serious. "Get real, Justice. We're talking about a baby. Babies disrupt routines. It's their nature."

"In that case, I'll expect you to keep the disruptions to a minimum."

She planted her hands on her hips and faced him down. "You're the one who insisted we come here, remember? If you can't handle the occasional disruption we'll leave."

"It's too late. We're about to get snow. A lot of it."

"I'm sure we can stay ahead of any incoming storms."

Justice jerked his head toward the window and Daisy's mouth dropped open. In the short time they'd been talking, ominous clouds had built up, sweeping over the mountain peaks and tumbling down the craggy slopes toward the ranch complex at an unbelievably rapid clip. Where in the world had that gorgeous expanse of pale blue sky gone?

He set Rumi on the table and took a final step toward her. Snagging her collar, he gave a swift tug, propelling her into his arms. "Three. I want to attempt to create a bond with you. To see if we can't form a family unit."

A bond. Family unit. How like him to describe something so intimate in such remote terms. "For Noelle's sake?"

He started to agree, but must have changed his mind at the last moment. "For all our sakes," he said instead.

"Even though I don't fit the parameters you created for a perfect apprentice/wife?"

"I suspect we'll both need to adjust our expectations since

I'm certain I don't fit your parameters, either. I'm willing to make the attempt if you are."

"And by 'bond' I assume that would include—" She started to say "making love" and took a quick verbal detour at the last instant. "Sex?"

Fire kindled in his golden gaze like wildfire. "Sex will be involved since it's one of the few places we seem able to communicate with perfect accord."

"Willing or not?" she dared to ask.

"Oh, you'll be willing. I guarantee it."

He cupped her face and lifted it for his kiss. She didn't resist. In truth, she didn't want to. He'd given her a delicious sample one short week ago, a sample that had reignited a passionate longing, as undeniable as it was overwhelming. She thought it had died long ago, but she'd been mistaken. Every time he reentered her life, he brought with him a want so intense, she didn't know how she'd survive if he didn't make her his again.

Beneath the icy exterior a fire burned, one fierce enough to melt any and all resistance. Did he realize what a dichotomy he represented with that ice-cold logical exterior and that white-hot inner blaze? He reminded her of a distant star, an inferno of heat within the cold vacuum of the space it occupied.

His mouth came down on hers and she sighed, opening to him with bottomless enthusiasm. His fingers tightened in her hair as he sank inward and she heard a faint rumble, almost like a cat's purr. Maybe she hadn't gotten it wrong in her books. Maybe at heart he really was like her jungle panther creation, Cat. While Cat hid behind a wall of protective foliage, Justice hid behind his icy demeanor and the isolated walls of his compound. Were they truly so different?

"What do you want from me?" Her question was smothered beneath his mouth.

But he caught the words. And he understood. Reluctantly,

he pulled back, pressing a searing kiss to the dampness of her lashes before taking her mouth a final time, a bittersweet tribute to the emotions he denied.

His thumbs traced the swollen contours of her mouth. "I want you."

"It's not that simple," she protested. "You treat whatever this is like it's a simple sexual equation. You plus me equals sex."

"It's just that simple."

She fought free of his hold, some of his iciness invading her own veins. "Is this really how you regard people in your life? Like simple equations? While you skate across the surface, never daring to plumb the depths?"

He turned away from her and reached for Rumi, freezing at the last instant. And that's when she saw it. Somehow, at some point during their earlier conversation, he'd transformed the device into a flower, one that looked remarkably like a daisy. She started to comment, then stopped, something warning her to tread carefully.

"I didn't realize it could do that," she commented, striving to sound casual and offhand.

"It's only happened once before." He spoke so quietly she almost didn't catch the words.

Before she could press him about it, Pretorius's voice erupted from hidden speakers. "Justice, who are those people in the kitchen?" He sounded almost frantic. "They're doing things in there. You need to stop them. Now."

"Take it easy," Justice replied. "I'll deal with it."

"You'll make them leave?"

"I'll deal with it."

At a guess, probably not the answer his uncle was looking for. "Cut communication," Justice ordered. He took a second to lock gazes with her. "This isn't over."

She lifted an eyebrow. "You're just figuring that out? Well, let's see if I can put this in terms that your computer-like brain will process…" She fisted her hand in his shirt and yanked until they were practically nose-to-nose. "I've known it wasn't over between us for nineteen months and twenty-five days. You didn't manage to figure it out until ten days ago and only when I showed up here to draw you a picture. Try to keep up from this point forward, okay?"

With that, she released him and swept from the room, though she could have sworn she heard a snort of laughter. Must have been the wind. Lord knew, it couldn't have been Justice. Together they returned to the kitchen…and walked in on sheer chaos.

"Son of a—"

She elbowed him. "Condition One alert."

"Look at what they've done to my kitchen!"

She couldn't blame him for being upset. She would have been, if it had been her home. Aggie had pulled everything out of the huge, walk-in pantry and stacked the contents on every available surface. A bucket of hot soapy water rested on the floor while she swabbed every shelf and cubbyhole.

Jett sat with her back to the doorway, earbuds plugged in and no doubt rocking out music at full blast. She pounded away at her laptop. Next to the laptop sat the cat, Kit, the other half of the inspiration for Daisy's storybook creations. She'd been freed from her carrier and reclined on the table, busily grooming herself, accepting the craziness around her with her usual equanimity. A computer's disembodied voice gave incomprehensible updates in a hiccuping voice, competing with Pretorius's shouted demands, demands that were interspaced with some truly creative obscenities.

And then there was Noelle. Daisy sighed.

All of the cupboard doors stood ajar. And her precious daughter sat buck naked in the middle of the floor surrounded by articles of baby clothing, along with every last pot and pan the kitchen possessed. She busily banged lids against pots adding to the noise level.

For an instant, Daisy thought Justice would explode. "Computer, disengage!"

"Disengaged."

Abruptly, silence reigned. Noelle paused in her banging, Jett in her typing. Aggie poked her head out of the pantry. One look at Justice and she flinched, knocking over her bucket of soapy water. It swirled in an ever-expanding puddle of suds heading toward Noelle.

Jett's fingers hovered over her laptop, mid-keystroke and her head jerked around. Her inky dark eyes widened in dismay when she saw Justice standing there. "Uh-oh."

Daisy hastened to pluck her daughter off the floor before the surge of dirty water reached her. "Darn it, Jett. You promised to behave."

Jett cleared her throat. "Actually, I didn't. You told me to. But since I didn't answer, technically I didn't promise anything."

"How many times have I warned you not to get technical with me?"

"Nineteen hundred and fifty-two."

"Enough!" Justice broke in, glaring around the room. "Someone tell me what the bloody *hell* is going on and I mean now."

Noelle beamed from the safety of her mother's arms and spoke her very first words to her father. "Hell!" she said, clear as a bell.

Daisy groaned. "Oh, that's just great. Which part of Condition One didn't you understand?"

"I possess perfect comprehension. This, however—" He swept his arm in a wide arc to encompass the disaster that had previously been his kitchen. "This defies even my ability to comprehend. But it's not beyond my ability to correct. First things first."

He waded through the water to the one drawer that had so far escaped Noelle's detection and remained intact. He upended the stack of dishtowels it contained onto the floor. Then he crossed to Jett's computer and with a few swift keystrokes disconnected her from his computer system.

"Full control returned to you, Pretorius."

"They're leaving now, right?"

"I'll be down shortly to discuss it."

"Discussing implies 'not leaving.' I don't want to discuss." A hint of panic crept into his voice. "I want them to leave."

"Give me five minutes. Computer disengage."

Then he turned his attention to his daughter and Daisy flinched. He'd allowed himself a quick look earlier, when they'd first arrived. A look, she didn't doubt, that had just about destroyed him. At a guess, he hadn't realized until that moment what sort of effect such a tiny human being could have on him. Well, he'd found out, and then some. He teetered on the edge of losing it, something she wouldn't allow to happen in front of so many witnesses.

"Aggie?" Daisy murmured. "Why don't you and Jett go on upstairs and pick out rooms."

"Would you like me to fix you a cup of hot tea before I go?" She spared Justice a warm smile. "I consider it the perfect restorative. No matter how upset I am, hot tea always makes me feel better."

"Later, perhaps."

The housekeeper's gaze shifted from Justice to Noelle and she gave a brisk nod of understanding. That quick comprehension was one of the qualities Daisy most admired about the former schoolteacher. Without another word, she gathered up Jett, and the two slipped from the room. Justice continued to stand, rooted in place, unable to take his eyes off his daughter. He started toward her and then hesitated. His usual forcefulness deserted him, exposing an unsettling vulnerability.

"May I?" he asked with painful formality.

Daisy swallowed against the tightness in her throat. "Of course. She's your daughter, too."

He approached Noelle and held out his hand. The move was so tentative and cautious it threatened to break Daisy's heart. Noelle grabbed his hand with her usual impulsiveness and yanked it to her mouth for a taste. Not giving him time to withdraw, Daisy transferred their daughter from her own arms to his. And then she stepped back, watching a connection form that no computer interface could duplicate.

Ever so gently, Justice settled his daughter into his arms, cradling her as though she might shatter, his grip a trifle awkward. She responded by touching everything within reach. If she could grab it, it went into her mouth for a taste. If she couldn't, her nimble fingers explored it as though attempting to discern how and why, where and what. And most important, whether she could take it apart.

"She's beautiful," he murmured.

"Thanks. I'd say it was the luck of the draw. Somehow I suspect you'd say something about the expression of genetic information and the role of dominant versus recessive versus blending genes," she dared to tease.

He glanced up, his eyes glittering with a hunger that threatened to bring her to her knees. How quickly it happened, that unbreakable bond that connected hearts and souls, parent to child. She caught the stamp of possession. The want. And even more, the need.

"Actually, I was about to say that she takes after you," he said.

Simple and sincere and utterly unlike Justice. It could only be Noelle's influence, and Daisy wished with all her heart that it wouldn't stop there. "I'd say she was a perfect blend. Look at her, Justice. Her eye color is somewhere between yours and mine. Her hair is more strawberry than blond or ebony. She's as extroverted as I am and as brilliant as you are."

As though in response to the comment, Noelle beamed at her father, showing off eight pearly nubs.

"She has teeth already." A slight frown creased Justice's brow. "And you said she's verbal. Can she walk?"

"Yes. She's still a little unsteady on her feet, but that doesn't stop her from getting to where she wants to go."

"So much," he murmured. "I've missed so much." He passed a hand over her curls, stroked a creamy cheek with his fingertip. She crowed in delight, grabbing his finger and tugging it back to her face. "She's not the least reticent."

"No, she has a very outgoing personality. She's never been at all clingy."

"Is she naked for a reason?"

Daisy wondered when he'd get around to that. "I'm afraid your daughter doesn't like wearing clothes. I don't know how she does it, but she's a little escape artist. I'll turn my back for no more than two seconds and she's wriggled out of whatever I've dressed her in. Cribs and high chairs don't hold her. And forget about a playpen."

"Huh."

"What does 'huh' mean?" she asked suspiciously.

He ignored her question. "And the cupboards?" he asked. "Was that your housekeeper or our daughter?"

Daisy sighed. "Noelle," she admitted.

"Huh."

She planted her hands on her hips. "That's twice you've 'huhed' your daughter and you still haven't explained the first one, let alone the second. What do you know that I don't?"

He hesitated, his eyes guarded, intensifying her level of concern. "My 'huh'—both of them—indicate a familiarity and understanding of Noelle's methods and thought processes."

She didn't bother to conceal her relief. "That didn't take long."

"No," he murmured. "But then, there's a reason for that."

"Please," she encouraged in a polite voice. "Don't keep it to yourself or I might just grab one of the pots Noelle was banging and beat it out of you."

Justice eyed her almost defensively. "I believe this might be the appropriate time to admit to a certain genetic propensity, one that I hope you'll learn to accept over time."

Her maternal instincts went on red alert. "You're making me very, very nervous. Are you suggesting there's something wrong with our daughter?"

"Not exactly."

"Then what? And I do mean exactly."

"It's not Noelle's fault. It's mine. It's part of the genetic makeup she inherited from me. How her brain is wired." He cradled Noelle tight against his body, very hard, the sweeping line of his posture telegraphing a clear protective impulse, one he'd no doubt deny if she dared point it out to him. "I would appreciate it if you wouldn't hold it against her."

"Hold it…" Daisy trailed off, stunned. "Dear God, Justice. Do you think I'd ever criticize our daughter for something as natural and basic as human curiosity? That I'd ever punish her for exploring her world and trying to figure out how it works?"

"Some people would. Some people would consider her flawed."

Hurt ripped through her, catching in her throat and bleeding through her words. "I'm not some people. I'm Noelle's mother. I adore her. I'd do anything for her. Sacrifice anything."

Justice closed his eyes and drew in a deep breath. "I apologize. It's just…" He looked at her again, direct and unflinching, his eyes the color of tarnished gold. "I've seen it happen before."

He made the statement so simply and resolutely, and yet with such unspeakable pain and vulnerability. Her heart ached for him. "Who did you see it happen to, Justice?" she asked gently. "You?"

He nodded. Once. "Noelle is processing her world by dismantling it," he explained. He paused a beat. Gathered himself. "That particular characteristic got me kicked out of my first half-dozen foster homes."

She didn't know what she'd expected, but it wasn't that. "Let me get this straight. Some of your earlier foster parents made you leave because you took things apart? Are you serious?"

"Quite." He clenched his jaw. "I tried not to. I did. But I couldn't seem to help myself. I imagine it became annoying when they'd get up in the morning, only to discover the coffeepot or toaster disassembled."

"Then, why did you do it?"

"I needed to take things apart and study them in order to understand how they worked." He made the statement as though it should have been obvious. "It was perfectly logical."

Daisy hid a smile. "Of course it was. Assuming you could then put them back together."

"That took a bit longer to master. Now that I think about it, your parents were the first to understand that." A small frown creased his brow, as though the memory were an unwelcome one. "I'd forgotten until now. Your father actually encouraged my curiosity by finding broken-down lawn mowers and computers and car engines and letting me tinker."

"I remember you had all these mechanical parts spread out over our entire garage," she murmured. "Everything organized just so on counters and tarps and in jars. And heaven help anyone who dared move so much as a single nut or bolt."

"And yet, you moved them all the time."

Her mouth tugged into a mischievous smile. "Only because it made you react. You were always so self-contained. My parents constantly told me to leave you alone. To respect your privacy."

"Not that you ever did."

"I couldn't," she admitted with a shrug. "While you were busy tinkering with mechanical puzzles, I couldn't resist deciphering a far more human one."

"My mistake with your parents was that I didn't confine my tinkering to the lawn mowers and computers and car engines." Unmistakable want burned a path across his face. "I had to take you apart, too."

Daisy sighed. "And some things, once taken apart, can't be put together again."

"Not the way they were before," he agreed.

She approached like a moth to a flame, drawn to the circle of heat and light formed by Justice and their daughter. "I swear to you, I didn't know they found out about us. I didn't know that's why you left. Why you were forced to go. I would have stood up for you if I had. I would have stopped them. Explained. Something."

He shook his head. "You were fifteen. There was nothing else to explain. Nor would standing up to them have changed anything. What we did was wrong and I paid the price for dismantling you."

"You shouldn't have had to."

"Yes, I should have. I realize that now." He glanced down at his daughter. "What would we do if it were Noelle at fifteen? If someone dismantled her at that age?"

Her breath caught. Shivered in her lungs. She couldn't begin to find the words to express what she felt and she could only stare at Justice in dismay.

"I agree," he said softly.

"Oh, Justice." Helpless. Hopeless. "What are we going to do?"

As usual, he had a plan. "First, I need to go downstairs and talk to Pretorius. He's going to have difficulty with the changes." Reluctantly, he handed over Noelle. "Afterward, I'd like to spend more time with our daughter, assuming that's acceptable to you."

"You don't need my permission." The fact that he felt he did distressed her. "You're her father. I'm here because it's important to me that you two bond."

He stared at his daughter and all expression winked from his face. "She's walking and talking, already. She has teeth. Are you certain it's not too late?"

Tears pricked Daisy's eyes. "No, Justice. It's not too late. Not if you don't let it be."

His gaze locked with hers and he gave a quick nod. "Then I won't let it be."

Seven

Daisy supposed she shouldn't be surprised that she couldn't sleep. It had been a long day, full of emotion. She'd seen Justice again after what felt like an endless separation. And Justice had finally met his daughter. That first tentative moment the two shared still brought tears to her eyes whenever she thought about it. It was far too early to determine whether she and Justice could live together on a permanent basis, though considering his third condition she hoped they stood a chance. But, she didn't have a single doubt he'd do everything within his power to be a father to Noelle. The bond she'd witnessed forming had been as immediate as it had been enduring.

She squirmed beneath the covers in an attempt to get more comfortable, but the glint of eyes from the corner of the nearly barren room snagged her attention. Kit was on the prowl. The cat slunk over to the bed and rumbled out a purr before leaping onto the mattress and giving Daisy a gentle head butt.

She scratched the cat behind the ears and was rewarded

with another thunderous purr. "So, what do you think of the new digs?" she whispered.

Not that she'd disturb anyone, even speaking in a normal voice. Justice had built a sturdy, solid house, and she couldn't help wonder if the impressive size stemmed from a subconscious imperative to fill it with a large family. Regardless, the walls and oak doors were heavy and thick enough that she could belt out Lady Gaga and they'd never hear her. Plus, Jett and Noelle had elected to "camp out" together in one of the massive bedrooms on the opposite side of the house, a room that overlooked a large pond, currently iced over and glittering with fresh fallen snow.

Instead of settling down at the end of the bed in her customary position, Kit's ears pricked up and her head swiveled toward the door. Tension swept through her sleek body and she went into predator mode. Slipping off the mattress, she made a beeline from the room.

Curious, Daisy gathered up the ankle-length cotton nightgown she wore, the warmest of her options, and followed the cat. The chill of oak flooring beneath her feet caused her to shiver. She reached the main level in time to catch a glimpse of Kit darting into forbidden territory.

Uh-oh. Did Justice's first condition—to keep everyone out of the basement—include the cat?

She hesitated at the top of the stairs leading to Justice's bat cave, debating whether or not to sneak down after Kit. She doubted the cat would come to any harm. Still… Who knew what Justice kept down there? There could be automated vacuums that might suck up a poor, defenseless cat. Electrified fences. Even killer robots.

Admit it, she silently scolded herself. Just admit that she couldn't sleep and wanted to talk to Justice to see if they had any chance at creating a lasting relationship. That she half hoped he would insist on giving her an intimate and thorough demonstration of Condition Three. Or she could confess she was dying of curiosity to take a peek at the forbidden. Concede the fact that she just couldn't resist stepping over whatever lines he drew in the figurative sand and never had been able to.

She surrendered to the inevitable, knowing full well she wouldn't sleep until she'd put a toe over that darned line of his.

Daisy reached the bottom step, that no-man's land between her territory and his, and stood there. Though she suspected the lower level occupied the same space as the floor above it, the setup was vastly different. Much more high-tech. The overhead lights were off, while low wattage lighting along the floor reflected off blindingly white walls and a crisp, almost sterile corridor. Leaning forward from the safety of the bottom step, she peered down a dimly lit hall to her right. Doorways sealed tightly shut led to mysterious rooms that she itched to explore.

"Now how did I know you'd break Condition One before the day was even over?"

Daisy jumped and her head jerked to the left. She wobbled on the step, catching her balance at the last possible second. "I haven't broken your condition." She offered an abashed grin. "Not yet."

He'd approached so silently she hadn't heard him. The subdued lighting of his underworld lair cast interesting shadows across his face, giving him a forbidding appearance. Okay, a more forbidding appearance. And yet for all that she found him appealing in the extreme. But then, she always had. She'd never understood it, never been able to adequately explain it. She just knew from the moment she first set eyes on the man he'd been the only one who did it for her on every possible level.

When Justice had left to go to college—or not to college, as she now knew—it had taken her years to get over what she'd assumed was an infatuation, that indelible mark left by her first love and lover. There had been other men in her life since, a select few. But they'd never stirred her the way Justice had. Never ignited that fierce fire that had quieted over the years, but never quite been doused. And since the night Noelle had been conceived, it had only grown worse. Intensified. Made her realize what they had was special and unique. More, she realized she wanted to be with him for as long as he'd allow it.

"What are you doing here?" he asked, the prosaic question making her smile.

"I'm on a rescue mission. Our cat came down here and I didn't know what sort of trouble Kit might get into."

"Kit?" He stilled, an odd expression shifting across his face. "As I recall, you named the kitten I gave you Kit. It was the night we made—"

He broke off, but she knew what he'd been about to say. The night they made love. Not "had sex" as he'd been so careful to label it since. Daisy let the silence stretch a moment before responding. "You said you chose Kit because we both had green eyes and were pure trouble."

"This can't be the same cat."

His adamant statement confused her, pricked her for some reason. She planted her hands on her hips and fixed him with a look of exasperation. "Of course it's the same cat, Justice. Didn't you recognize her?"

"I didn't even realize you brought a cat," he confessed. "I guess my focus was elsewhere."

She softened, feeling a tug on her heartstrings. "Yes, of course it was. You couldn't take your eyes off your daughter."

"Or you."

He approached with the silent grace she'd always associated with him. Thanks to her position on the step, they stood eye-to-eye, the odd dark gold of his gaze gathering up the light and hinting at wonders and mysteries and delicious depths to be plumbed. They also glimmered with an odd emotion, one she couldn't quite pinpoint.

"You kept the cat I gave you for all these years?" He phrased the question almost like an accusation, as though determined to force her to deny it.

Indignation swept through Daisy. "Did you think I'd throw her out?" she asked. "I adore her."

Adored her in part because he'd given her the cat, though she didn't dare admit as much. But also because she'd formed an immediate attachment to the mischievous little beast, one that continued to this day. Kit was part of her family. Part of her life. And a lifeline that remained to this day, connecting the two of them through all the years stretching between them.

"I thought your parents might get rid of her." He shrugged. "All things considered."

"You mean because they threw you out, they'd throw your cat out, too?"

His expression closed down. "Something like that."

"Well, they didn't," Daisy retorted. "She's been with me for ten years now. If I'm lucky, she'll be with me for another ten. Didn't you notice I used her in my storybooks?"

Clearly, he hadn't made the connection. "So, she really is Kit, both in reality and in fiction," he murmured.

"Yes, she is. And in case you didn't catch it… You're Cat."

"The panther?" His eyes darkened. "That's me?"

"It seemed fitting at the time." She smiled, daring to tease. "So are you going to let me use Kit as an excuse for a tour of the forbidden?"

"If I satisfy your curiosity, will you stay out?"

"I'll try."

He released a sigh and held out his hand. "Come on."

She stepped into the hallway, the tile even icier than the wood flooring. She suppressed a shiver, not wanting to give

Justice any excuse to send her away. "What's down that way?" She pointed to the right.

"That's my uncle's section. You don't get a tour of that area without his express invitation." He paused, capturing her chin within the warmth of his palm and tipping it up. "I'm serious, Daisy. You have to allow him his privacy. No stray cats. No sneaking down in the middle of the night. No excuses. Got it?"

"I wouldn't do that," she assured him. "Honestly, I wouldn't. I might give you a hard time because I know you can take it. But not Pretorius."

Her sincerity must have come through loud and clear. He gave a single sharp nod, then gestured to the left. "I have a number of labs down this way, as well as my private quarters."

Good Lord. "A *number* of labs?"

He shrugged. "For measurement and instrumentation. Another for research and development. A computer lab. A test lab. It isn't as specialized as the Sinjin complex, but it works well enough for tinkering."

"I want to see the robot lab."

He actually grinned. "Okay. I'll let you see the nonsterile one."

"You have sterile labs?"

"Yes, but you have to be naked and sterilized before you can go in."

One look assured he was kidding. Excellent. She'd only been here a few hours and she'd already infected him with a sense of humor. "It must not do a very good job sterilizing," she retorted. "Otherwise you wouldn't have a daughter."

He placed his palm against a plate outside one of the doors and then requested admittance. "Maybe we don't have to be sterilized," he admitted while they waited for his security system to run his palm and voiceprint.

"And maybe we don't have to be naked, either?"

The door to the lab slid silently open. "No, I'm pretty much going to insist on nudity."

She stepped into a huge room that looked very much like a workshop. Long tables spanned one half of the room and lined the walls. Predictably, they were a crisp, painful white. Instrumentation—none of which she recognized—clustered in a half-dozen stations perched on top of various tables. Each station also possessed its own computer system. At the opposite end of the room were endless cabinets and shelves and banks of drawers, most on rollers. Supplies, at a guess. Everything was ruthlessly organized which didn't come as much of a surprise considering Justice's propensity for neatness.

Dead center in the middle of the room stood a huge, sturdy workbench, possibly the messiest section of the room, not that Daisy found it all that messy. To her amusement, one of his Rumi spheres had been left there, and like the one in the office, this one had been transformed into a daisy, as well. She started to comment on that fact, then thought better of it, something in his expression warning her to tiptoe around that particular subject. Instead, she turned her attention to his work project.

Resting on the table squatted two odd devices on treads, presumably to give them mobility. She studied the first which combined dark metal and light gray plastic in a round shape the approximate size of a canister vacuum cleaner. Specialized arms spoked the device and what looked like a ring of aquamarine eyes dotted the circumference. A small helmet capped it, the helmet studded with lights and buttons and a display screen. Beside it squatted its more sophisticated twin.

"What are they?" she asked, fascinated.

"That's Emo X-14 and X-15. Short for Emotibot, X for the tenth generation, fourteenth and fifteenth versions." Justice frowned. "At least, that's what they're supposed to be. Right now they aren't much of anything."

"What are you hoping they'll become?" She shot him a questioning look. "Is that a better way to phrase it?"

"Much better, I'm afraid." He blew out a sigh. "Eventually I'm hoping Emo will be the next generation lie detector. A feeling detector, I suppose."

She stared at the robots, intrigued by the idea. "Why would you want to create a feeling detector?"

"I'm attempting to design a robotic that can anticipate and respond to human needs, not just based on what is requested verbally, but also to nonverbal cues. In fact, I'd like to use the in-house videos and cameras to photograph everyone's various emotion responses to stimuli over the next several weeks in order to help teach it. Assuming none of you objects."

"Huh." Intriguing. "I'll check with the others, but I have no objection. So, let me get this straight. By using photos and videos of us coming unhinged, or whatever, Emo will figure out when we're happy or sad or hungry or thirsty and do something about it?"

"Exactly." A smile danced across his mouth. "Although it isn't necessary for you to come unhinged in order to teach it appropriate emotional responses."

Daisy waved that aside. "That is *so* cool." For some reason she was drawn to the less sophisticated model, perhaps because the haphazard appearance gave it a bit more personality than its starkly streamlined big brother. "And this little guy can do some of that already? He can process emotional responses?"

Justice grimaced. "No, this little guy cannot do that, which is the current problem. Emo 14 hasn't been as successful at reading emotions as 15. I may have to scrap this particular model and repurpose its parts."

"Oh, no," Daisy protested. "He's too adorable to scrap."

One look warned he'd shifted into remote, logical scientist mode. "Adorable or not, sometimes when there's a catastrophic failure and what you're attempting to produce isn't working on any level, you just have to scrap it and start over."

Logical, as always, but still... "I hope you won't do that with 14."

Justice lifted an eyebrow. "Why not?"

She caught her lip between her teeth. "I don't know. He's so cute...it seems mean, somehow."

"Mean," he repeated. "Daisy, Emo is a machine, not a 'he.' It's not sentient. It'll never be sentient. If I anthropomorphized every one of my creations, I'd never get anything accomplished."

"I guess. Although you did name it. What's that if not anthropomorphizing a machine?" To her private amusement, he winced, her point finding its mark. Satisfied, she continued. "I know Emo isn't alive. It's just that he reminds me of something you were working on ten years ago."

He stilled. "You remember that?"

"Of course, I remember it. I found all your creations fascinating." She pulled out one of the stools tucked under the workbench and perched on the padded seat. Anything to get her poor abused feet off the cold floor. "But my favorite was the one that reminds me of Emo. The spaceship on rollers."

"It wasn't a spaceship."

"Yes, I know." She didn't know whether to laugh or roll her eyes. "You told me that a thousand times. But it looked like one and it somewhat resembles this little guy."

"Actually, it's the other way around. This little guy resembles the spaceship, as you call it. That's because it's the prototype for Emo. I work on the project in my spare time."

"I'm surprised you haven't finished it after so many years." His expression closed over and she wondered what she'd said to upset him. Because there wasn't a doubt in her mind that she'd struck a nerve. "But I guess you have to give the paying projects priority," she hastened to add.

"Yes." A hint of bleakness crept into his voice.

Somehow she'd opened a door she shouldn't have and she didn't have a clue how to close it again. "What's wrong, Justice?"

He turned away. How did she do it? How did she slip beneath his guard with such ease? For as long as he'd known her, she'd possessed that uncanny knack. And for as long as he'd known her, it had thrown him off-kilter. With that glorious fall of wheat-blond hair and those sparkling green eyes, she could short-circuit his brain with a single smile. In all the years he'd known her, he'd never figured out why the hell he didn't affect her the way he did every other person in existence, why she chased instead of ran.

He'd discovered at a young age that his appearance and intellect intimidated people, even his parents to a certain extent. They'd never understood the cuckoo who had appeared in their nest, though he'd later learned that he took after his father's brother, Pretorius, another strike against him considering his uncle's social anxiety issues. His parents' death in the car accident when he'd been all of ten had thrown him into foster care and prompted him to use that knowledge to hold people at a safe distance, often with a single, dark look.

But not Daisy. Never Daisy. No matter how many black looks he gave her, she remained impervious. No matter how many lines he drew, whether virtual or actual, she wriggled that potent little body across them as though they didn't exist. Even now, sitting in his workshop in a nearly transparent nightgown she managed to fit in when she should have been as out of place as an ice sculpture in the fiery bowels of hell.

He remembered when he'd first moved in with the Marcellus family, Daisy had invaded his room and his life like a dizzying spring breeze, both relentlessly determined and passionately warm. He hadn't wanted to be invaded, so he set boundaries, literal ones. He'd taped lines on the rug, blocking off his personal sections of the house, lines she'd taken great delight in yanking up and moving until he'd discover his personal space encompassing smaller and smaller areas. In the end, he'd been left with tiny boxes that would barely contain a mouse. Daisy simply refused to be shut out.

She still refused to be shut out, whether from his thoughts or his emotions or even his career. Somehow she managed to sweep into his life and lock herself around him with all the brilliance and delightful joie de vivre that was such an innate part of her. As a callow teenager, he'd been unable to defend or resist. And now...

Now, nothing had changed.

Surrendering to the inevitable, Justice joined her at the workbench and touched the panel on the robot's helmet. Instantly, Emo 14 hummed to life, a series of lights twinkling gaily. "Emo, this is Daisy."

"Hello, Daisy," a sweetly youthful male voice said.

She was instantly enchanted. "Hello, Emo."

"How are you feeling today?"

To his amusement, she gave the question serious consideration. She shot Justice a glance from beneath a sweep of lashes. "I'm feeling a little nervous and a bit upset at the idea that your creator might dismantle you."

"Perhaps you simply require a restorative cup of Aggie's hot tea," Justice suggested.

She narrowed her magnificent eyes in clear displeasure. "Perhaps I do."

Emo's lights twinkled and she caught a muted hum, somewhat similar to the sound Jett's laptop made when it accessed a program. "Processing," Emo informed her, his voice giving a little hiccup.

Daisy frowned. "Or perhaps Emo needs some tea. What's with his hiccup?"

Justice grimaced. "It happens sometimes when he—*it*—is running multiple functions."

A quick, appealing smile winged free. "He can't walk, talk and process at the same time?"

"Not very well."

She patted the robot's helmet. "He's still young. Give him time." A small frown formed between her brows. "You're not going to kill him off just because he's a little slow, are you?"

Kill him? Justice scrubbed his hands across his face. "I'm going to say this one more time, Daisy. I would appreciate it if you would pay close attention. Emo is a machine. You can't kill a machine."

At the sound of its name, Emo perked up. "How do you feel?" he chirped.

She shot Justice a look of supreme indignation. "I'm very, very sad, Emo. Sad enough that I may just have to wake Aggie and ask her to fix me a cup of tea. And it's all your maker's fault."

Justice held up his hands in surrender. "Okay, okay. I won't dismantle Emo. Instead of giving his parts to a future sibling, I'll keep him for the sake of posterity. Happy now?" Dear God, now she had him calling Emo "he" and "him." How did she do it? And how the hell did he fight against it?

"Yes, I'm happy now. Thank you."

She hesitated and he waited her out. "There's something I've been meaning to discuss with you."

"I'm not going to like this discussion, am I?"

"Doubtful." Not that that stopped her. "We need to hire some people to come in and scrub the upper two floors. It's not fair to dump this level of cleaning on Aggie, Jett and me." Then she got really nasty. "More importantly, having the house in this condition isn't healthy for Noelle."

"Son of a—"

"Condition One."

"Gun." He glared at her. "You are the most irritating woman—"

"Condition Two."

"—I have ever met. And if you don't stop spouting conditions at me, we'll go elsewhere and have a thorough and comprehensive discussion of my third condition. Are we clear?"

To his satisfaction, bright color burned a path across her elegant cheekbones. "Crystal."

"Excellent." He made an adjustment to Emo's control panel while he considered. "As for the cleaning problem, of course you can hire anyone you need to help. It's important you be comfortable here."

"What about your uncle?"

He gave it a moment's consideration. "I'll have Pretorius run a comprehensive system diagnostic scan during the cleaning process. That will take us offline for almost half a day, which knocks out his eyes and ears, and should prevent him from realizing anyone has been in the house until they've already left. Will that be sufficient, do you think?"

"Thank you. That should be perfect."

One quick glance warned she wasn't finished. "Another issue?" he asked mildly.

Daisy cleared her throat. "Not an issue, exactly."

"Please. Let's be exact."

"It's about your house."

"Is there something wrong with my house other than the level of cleanliness?"

"Yes. There isn't any place to sit."

Justice frowned. His one foray into the apprentice/wife waters had been with Pamela, a huge mistake, riddled with compatibility issues. Far from being the perfect fit the Pretorius Program assured him they'd be, they were perfectly imperfect for one another. After Pamela's departure, he'd cleared out the upper levels she'd furnished and decorated. With the exception of his office, he rarely visited them and hadn't bothered to replace any of the furniture. "No, I guess there isn't."

"We'd like to sit," Daisy said gently. "And, oh, I don't know, a few extra beds and dressers wouldn't go amiss."

"Would you be willing to order the necessary furniture?"

"You don't object? Considering the size of this place, it could get pricey."

"Will it cost more than nine-point-seven-three billion?"

To his amusement, she thought it through before replying. "I'm pretty sure I can keep the expenses under that."

"Then I don't object."

"Thank you."

Escaping her perch, she approached, her nightgown swirling around her, clinging to intriguing curves just long enough to give him a visual taste before billowing free, leaving him longing for another glimpse. Longing for a touch. Longing to have her in his arms and in his bed one more time and discover if what they'd experienced those previous occasions had been fluke or the norm. Although, he readily conceded, there'd been nothing in the least normal about Daisy or what happened between them whenever they made love.

Finally, she spoke. "There's something else bothering me."

"Other than the cleaning and furnishings?"

"Yes." She caught her lower lip between her teeth. "Do you really believe that when you experience a catastrophic failure and what you're attempting to produce isn't working on any level, you just have to throw it away and start over?"

"Yes."

She spared him a brief, hesitant look. "You could say that our relationship experienced a catastrophic failure."

Huh. He hadn't considered it that way. "I would consider that an accurate description."

"So would I," she confessed. "And the morning after we made love you did throw our relationship away, at least the potential for a relationship."

She was killing him, bit by bit. "I tried."

"Maybe now we can start over, dig beneath our surface attraction. Maybe we could repurpose the good parts and get it right this time. Because there were good parts, occasions when we communicated quite brilliantly."

He didn't pretend to misunderstand. "I believe you called it amazing."

"I believe I did." She moistened her lips, the only sign of her uncertainty. "What do you say, Justice?"

He couldn't resist her now any more than he could ten years ago. Or even nineteen months, twenty-six days, seven hours and two minutes ago. For the first time in his entire life he didn't hesitate. Didn't ponder and consider. He simply jumped, grabbed. Held on for all he was worth.

"I'd like that," he said gruffly. He pulled her into his arms. She walked into the embrace and enclosed him in softness and warmth. "How are you feeling?" he whispered against her mouth.

"Hungry. Very, very hungry."

Justice swept Daisy into his arms and carried her from the lab. The sheer cotton of her nightgown fluttered around them as though dancing beneath a wayward breeze. It clung to the shape of her, allowing the sheen of pearly skin to seep through the material while obscuring the details. Not for long. He intended to have her in his bed and naked within the next thirty seconds. Less, if at all possible.

He shouldered open the door to his bedroom. "Lights," he ordered. "Low wattage."

The bedside table lights flickered to life, sending a soft glow across her features. She was so beautiful, her eyes a deep, shadowed green, reflecting an unstinting passion. So open. So generous. So giving.

He realized in that endless moment that he didn't want to rush. Time no longer held any meaning, which he found vaguely bewildering. All that mattered was giving her pleasure. He set her on the bed and came down beside her. Cupping her face, he lifted it to his. And then he took her mouth. He held himself back, intent on making each second as memorable as possible. A quiet sigh escaped her, one of sheer joy, and in that moment he felt a happiness and contentment he hadn't experienced since the last time he had her in his arms and in his bed.

Maybe it was because of the extent of his own satisfaction that he realized he couldn't make love with her under the current circumstances. When they came together it wouldn't be due to conditions or obligation, but because it was what they both wanted.

Even so, that didn't keep him from stroking the curve of her cheek before drawing back. "You don't have to stay, if you'd rather not. I rescind my third condition."

Laughter glittered in her eyes. "I really wish you wouldn't."

She'd taken him by surprise. "No?"

"Definitely not. Because then I won't be forced to sacrifice my virtue and might feel obligated to leave."

Her clear amusement drew a smile from him. "I gather you don't want to leave?"

"Not in the least."

"You're willing to sacrifice your virtue?"

"Well…if you insist." She drew him into the soft heat of her embrace. "Please insist," she whispered against his mouth.

"In that case, I rescind my rescission and insist that you let me have my wicked way with you." He nibbled at her lower lip. "Most definitely insist."

She released her breath in an exaggerated sigh. "Since I have no other choice, I'm all yours. But I expect you to keep your promise and be wicked with me. Very, very wicked."

He swept a hand along her cheek again, then lower. God, her skin was like satin. "Whatever I want?"

"If you need a few suggestions, I'm happy to provide them."

"I think I have it covered," he informed her gravely. "But if there's anything that will make your sacrifice more bearable, don't hesitate to let me know."

She slanted him a sparkling look. "Perhaps another kiss will help me tolerate it a little better?"

"A kiss like this…?"

He took her mouth again, allowing his passion to slip his control ever so slightly. She sighed in appreciation and her lips parted, surrendering to him, before matching him kiss for kiss.

"It's different this time, isn't it?" she asked him.

He tucked a silky swathe of hair behind her ear. "Different how?"

She regarded him with unusual gravity and all the while her hands fluttered across him like butterflies. They constantly touched and stroked, anchoring him to her in some indefinable, yet permanent manner. "The first time we made love we were children and I was pretending to be someone I wasn't," she explained. "The second time you thought I was someone I wasn't. But this time…"

He understood then. "It's real. It's honest. You know who I am and I know who you are."

She nodded. "I like it better this way."

"So do I."

And he did. It added a deeper dimension to their love-making. Strengthened the connection between them. Unable to resist, he eased the soft cotton of her nightgown from her shoulders only to find even softer skin beneath, pliant and warm and responsive. He traced her curves, familiarizing himself with the subtle changes motherhood had wrought.

Even that bound them together, a deep, irreversible connection he couldn't break even if he felt so inclined. They'd created a child together, would always be linked through their daughter. For the rest of their lives they'd have that in common. And if they were fortunate, Noelle would only be the start.

Their mouths collided again, more urgently this time, and the mattress cushioned their tumble, their arms and legs entwining, clinging with a growing urgency. A prelude to what was to come. Without the least trace of uncertainty or artifice, she broke free and came up on her knees. With a grace she'd possessed even as an untried teen, she swept her nightgown up and over her head and allowed it to drift to the floor. She continued to kneel before him, utterly vulnerable in her nudity and in the unstinting way she gifted herself to him. That openness and generosity of spirit was such an innate part of her.

And it never failed to impress the hell out of him.

The bedside lamp cast a gentle glow across her, sweeping over the fullness of her breasts before sliding coyly into the shadowed juncture of her thighs. Her skin made him think of virginal snow, yet offered the vibrancy of new life. And he wanted her. All of what she offered. Wanted her more than he thought possible.

She represented everything he wasn't. Everything he lacked. She was the hope of an everlasting spring who'd somehow invaded the dark desolation of winter. She was Persephone, surrendering to Hades.

"Stop," she murmured. He jerked back, steeling himself to let her go, no matter how difficult. She sighed, reached for him, drew him closer and enclosed him in warmth. "I don't mean stop touching me. I mean stop thinking. Stop analyzing. Just let go and feel, Justice."

"I don't think I can do anything else," he admitted. Or maybe it was a confession. "Not with you."

Gently, tenderly, he wrapped himself around her and kissed her with a passion that left her gasping for breath.

Desire brought heat storming across her skin, tinting the paleness with the soft flush of need. He cupped her breast, took the tip in his mouth and anointed it with tongue and teeth. He could feel the pounding of her heart against his cheek and the soft moan that shuddered from her lungs, a moan that carried his name.

She shifted against him, her legs parting, hips lifting and meshing with his. He'd wanted to take his time, to reacquaint himself with every inch of her. "Next time," he promised, though he had no idea if she understood.

Or maybe she did because she laughed. "Okay, next time we'll go slow. But not now. Now I want all of you. Fast."

She flowed around him, gripping and stroking, taking, then giving. His hands tripped across trembling thighs, cupping the silky backs and angling them upward. Then he sank into her soft, fluid warmth. Her moans turned to sobs, frantic and pleading, and he drove into her, desperate to drive her to peak. To please her. Satisfy her in every way possible.

He saw it in her eyes an instant before she climaxed, right before he followed her over the top. The brilliant desire. The burgeoning. And he saw something else. Something that threatened to destroy him. In those stunning green eyes he saw the one thing he'd never trusted. Never dared believe in.

He saw love.

Eight

Oh, no. What had she done?

Daisy closed her eyes and burrowed against Justice, hiding her expression from him. Too fast and too soon, came the helpless thought.

This time round she'd planned to take their relationship at a slow, steady clip, instead of with her usual exuberance. This time she'd hoped to allow their feelings time to develop and mature slowly. Fully. To grow at a reasonable pace that encompassed the intellectual and rational, rather than just the emotional. To reach the point where they could make a commitment to one another on every level, not just a sexual one.

She suppressed a tearful laugh. So much for that plan. It hadn't even lasted twenty-four short hours before she'd flung herself into Justice's arms and bed, just as she had every other time she'd been within kissing distance of the man. And why? Because it was the one place where they'd always been in perfect accord. The place where she hoped their relationship could take seed and flower into something deeper and more meaningful.

But in order for that seed to flourish, it meant Justice would have to make an emotional commitment to her. And at this point, she didn't know whether he even recognized that he possessed emotions. She'd seen them, been stunned by the depths of them—when they'd made love. When he held his daughter. On rare, bittersweet occasions when she caught him looking at her.

But considering the depth of his disconnect, she doubted he'd made the connection. Maybe if he managed to get his robots up and running they could explain it to him. Of course, he probably wouldn't believe them. He'd probably think they still weren't working right, and dismantle them in order to repurpose the parts for an Emo model X-Trillion and Two.

"Daisy?" he murmured. "Are you all right?"

"Not really." She needed to distract him, find a way to disguise how fast and hard she'd tumbled. To give him the time he would need to consider and analyze and explain away the emotions that locked them together over time and circumstance, before surrendering to the inevitable. She forced a smile to her lips and peeked up at him, forcing a teasing tone to her voice. "I'm a little confused about one of the sub clauses to your third condition. Perhaps if you explained it to me in a bit more detail?"

To her delight, he chuckled, more relaxed than she'd ever seen him. "Which sub clause didn't you understand?" He slid his hand along her leg until he wandered onto territory blessed by soft, feminine warmth. "This clause…?"

"That's one." She returned the favor, stroking her hand along the length of him, a territory neither soft nor feminine. "And I do believe this is another."

"Ah. Now that particular clause I can explain in explicit detail."

She smiled, keeping her tone light, though her jumbled emotions spilled recklessly free, refusing any attempts at restraint. "I'd like that," she told him. "I'd like that very much."

First thing the next morning, Daisy made a firm promise to herself that she'd take her relationship with Justice at a slower, more decorous pace. That she'd hide her feelings from him until he'd had time to assimilate or analyze or cogitate or whatever mad scientists did in order to reach their ridiculous conclusions regarding issues that should be perfectly straightforward and obvious.

Like love.

Of course, her vow lasted right up until he took her into his arms the next night. This time he swept her off to her upstairs bedroom. Once there, clothed only in honesty, her true feelings escaped her ability to control. Unbidden and unhidden, they exploded from her, as clear and brilliant as sunlight, while Justice's remained cloaked in shadows. And over the subsequent nights they spent in her bed, Daisy continued to hope he'd eventually surrender to his feelings instead of hiding behind his rationality and logic and the darkness of past memories. But instead, he left her bed each morning to return to his underground lair before the first rays of daylight dared penetrate the room.

In the meantime, she arranged for the cleaning crew to scrub the house from top to bottom. As promised, Justice requested his uncle run a complete housewide diagnostic scan. Not that it worked as planned. No sooner had the cleaners departed than Pretorius came online, his voice booming through the speakers.

"Justice? Justice! Red alert. One of the units has gone off the grid. I need a head count right away."

"Everything's fine, Pretorius," came Justice's calm response. "I'm in the kitchen with Aggie, Daisy and Noelle."

"There's still one missing," Pretorius shot back, then couldn't prevent himself from dipping into sarcasm. "Or have you forgotten how to count?"

"Would you like a nice cup of hot tea?" Aggie asked in a motherly voice. "You sound upset."

"No, I would not like some hot tea," Pretorius snapped. "I want to know where the other one is. The troublemaker. She's missing."

"I'm not missing. I'm right here."

Pretorius erupted out of his chair and spun around. Jett sat curled like a cat on the counter behind him. Panic caused his heart to race and he fought to control his breathing. He tugged at the collar of his Metallica T-shirt, feeling cold sweat pool at the base of his spine. "What the hell are you doing down here?" he demanded tightly.

Only her eyes moved, a quick blink over intense, dark irises. "You and Justice sure swear a lot," she commented in such a cool, matter-of-fact voice that he felt some of his panic ease.

"You haven't answered my question, little girl. What are you doing here?"

"First, I'm not a little girl. I'm sixteen."

He snorted and shoved his glasses higher on the bridge of his nose. "Try twelve."

Her eyes narrowed, but she let that pass. "I figured since the computer was offline you'd lose your eyeballs and I could sneak down here and watch you for a change. Since you're always watching us, it only seemed fair."

To his utter shock, he felt a blush warm his cheeks. "Justice tell you not to come down here? That I don't like people, so you should stay away?"

"Yeah." Jett frowned. For the first time a hint of uncertainty crept across her pixielike features. "But I figured I wasn't exactly like real people."

"Well, you are." His frown matched hers, grew to a scowl.

"Why don't you think you're like real people?" he asked, driven despite himself to ask the question.

Jett shrugged. "Everybody always said so."

"Oh, yeah? I got news for you. Everybody's full of sh—" Pretorius broke off and he stabbed a stubby finger in her direction. "Take my word for it. You're real people. I should know. I can't abide real people and since I can't abide you, that makes you real."

His rudeness didn't faze her in the least. She simply nodded. For some reason her stoic acceptance of his remark bothered him more than he thought possible. "I was thinking since I bug you so much, you could pretend I was one of Justice's robotics or something." She focused on him, her expression carefully blank. "That's what they called me, you know. Faulty Chip. Like a computer chip because I was so smart and logical, but faulty because I didn't get all freaked and worked up like the rest of them over every little thing. Wasn't emotional enough to suit them."

"They really called you that?" Pretorius couldn't seem to get past her single, painfully composed statement.

"It's okay." She lifted a shoulder in a shrug that was meant to appear uncaring. Instead it made her seem unbearably young and vulnerable. "Anyway, I was thinking… Maybe if you thought of me like that, like a robot or something, you know? I could hang out down here sometimes and watch you work. Pick up a few pointers."

"Well, you can't. I don't like people. They make me nervous."

"You don't look nervous. You just look ticked." Jett tilted her head to one side. "Maybe if you let me come around every once in a while, you won't be so nervous or ticked anymore. Maybe you'd even learn to like me."

He'd spent years listening to people, observing them from a safe distance. The practice had honed his ears and eyes to the point that he caught the merest hint of nerves slipping through her voice. A desperate want. And though she tried to control it, he also saw the wistful hope that tumbled across the youthful planes of her face. He opened his mouth to reject her and found he couldn't speak the crushing words. Couldn't be one more person in her life to rebuff her. Didn't have the heart to send her away. Besides, for some reason she didn't make him quite as nervous as most people.

"Okay, you can stay for a bit," he grudgingly agreed. "But the minute I get nervous, you're out of here."

Her eyes lit with excitement, glittering like the semi-precious stone for which she'd been named. She fought to keep tight control over the explosion of emotions others had been foolish enough to believe she didn't experience. "Thanks, Uncle P. I'll just sit here real quiet and stay out of your way. You'll never know I'm here."

The "Uncle P." almost did him in. "Sit there? Not a chance. You hang down here, you gotta pull your weight."

"Really?" Her joy was so painfully intense that he had to look away before he did something unmanly. Like blubber.

"Yes, really." He kicked the spare office chair in her direction. It shot across the floor toward her, the castors rattling noisily. "Well? What are you waiting for. Get down here and show me some of your computer moves." He curled his lip in the best sneer he could manage. "Assuming you have any."

She erupted from the counter and bounced into the seat, scooting over beside him. "You're on."

The next week furniture showed up from a local manufacturer whose work Daisy admired. And she hired a huge mountain of a man, Cord, to oversee the various alterations. They were along the line of minor tweaks, since Justice had built an excellent house with fabulous bone structure. It just needed a few cosmetic touches to take it from a house to a home. Well, tweaks and furniture.

"That's all I'm trying to do," she explained to Justice when he confronted her about the "tweaks." "Create a home for all of us."

"Fine. I get that part. But does the creative process have to be so damn noisy?" Instantly a shrill *wheep* sounded from the speakers. His brows pulled together. "And what the bloody hell—" *Wheep!* "—was that?"

Daisy winced. "First, yes, the creative process of transforming a house into a home has to be noisy. I promise it won't be for much longer. And I think you'll be quite pleased with the results."

One look at her anxious expression and he caved. "I'm sure I will be pleased," he reluctantly agreed. "And that noise?"

Oh, dear. She twisted her hands together. "Jett is running an experimental program."

"Not any longer she isn't." Justice frowned, and she could practically see him rewinding her explanation and homing in on the one detail she hoped would escape his notice. She should have known better. "What sort of experimental program?"

Daisy cleared her throat. "I believe it's a behavioral modification program."

It only took him a single heartbeat to add two and two. But then, Justice had always been excellent at math. "Are you telling me she's created a program that emits that…that *noise* whenever I swear?"

Daisy flinched at the outrage in his voice. "I'll speak to her."

"You're damn—" *Wheep!* "—right you'll speak to her. I want that program terminated by the end of the day."

"And the other changes?" she dared to ask, gesturing toward the great room.

They'd made serious headway over the past few days. The great room, as well as the dining room, was beginning to assume the function and appearance for which they'd been

intended. The walls were still a painful white, but she'd
address those in short order.

Justice stepped into the great room and studied the huge
high-ceilinged expanse. She'd opened the shutters covering
the picture windows to allow in a glorious view of winter
landscape. The furniture she'd ordered was solid, yet elegant.
Simple, yet comfortable. The textures and colors practically
cried out, "Sit on me. Relax. Enjoy a conversation with
friends and neighbors."

Dead center in front of the picture window she'd put up
a Christmas tree. Though Cord had strung it with colorful
fairy lights that twinkled merrily, they'd yet to decorate it.
She hoped to involve the entire family in the activity. Best
of all, she'd found a mischievous cherubic angel to top the
tree, the bright golden-red curls and beaming face uncannily
similar to Noelle's.

"It's lovely, Daisy," Justice said gruffly.

"Really? You like it?"

He tugged her into his arms. Since her arrival—and their
lovemaking—he'd been more open and demonstrative in his
affections. He was trying, no question about that. They just
needed time. Time to become accustomed to each other. Time
to settle into a routine. Time to learn to open up and trust.

To love.

There in front of the Christmas tree he kissed her and in
that perfect moment she realized she was vanquished. She'd
lost her heart to him when she'd been little more than a child.
And though her feelings had been those of a child, they'd
been the wellspring for what she now felt. What she hoped
he'd also feel, given time. She had no idea what wonderful
fate had caused them to cross paths again, or what accident
of nature had occurred that ended in Noelle's conception and
birth, but she would be eternally grateful.

"I always have done everything backward," she murmured dreamily. "Jumping first and looking afterward when it was far too late."

He glanced at the tree, at the room, and smiled. "Funny. I would have said you did it perfectly."

Well, perfect or not, now that she'd gotten Justice on board, it was time to address a final serious imperfection. As one day flowed into the next, Daisy couldn't take it any longer. All these white walls were driving her insane. It was almost as though they taunted her. *You've lost it. You'll never paint again.* Even though she'd set up her studio, she still couldn't work. She wouldn't accept those heartbreaking whispers. She couldn't. If she started believing them, she'd go insane.

Besides, ever since coming here, something wondrous had happened. She'd felt a…a burgeoning. A stirring of new life not unlike what she'd experienced while pregnant with Noelle. Her hands itched to wrap around a brush. She longed for the messy mix and slide of paints. Of endless colors filling her palette. The scent of linseed oil. The texture, thick and rich and dense. The soft, wet skate of brush against canvas. The growth of a dream from first stroke to last.

She glared at the walls. Canvas. White wall. What was the difference? It didn't matter one bit so long as it gave birth to the dream.

It didn't take long to find the case containing her supplies. She selected a brush, stunned when that one simple action caused tears to fill her eyes. It had been so long. So unbelievably long. An endless winter of creative barrenness. Careful now, trying not to raise her expectations too high, she selected her paints while tears tracked her cheeks, a bewildering combination of joy and fear.

She'd start slow, she decided, swiping the dampness from her face. Small. Just something whimsical to get herself started. Something Justice would never notice…

* * *

Justice halted in his tracks and glared at a section of wall near where Noelle sat playing. "What the bloody he—*heck* is that?" he demanded.

"Hell," Noelle happily prattled.

"Please don't swear in front of our daughter," Daisy said automatically. She strove for Noelle-like innocence and fell somewhat short. "And what is what?"

"Da—*darn* it! It's practically winter. Pretorius?"

Noelle clapped her hands together and crowed. "P.P!"

The hidden speakers crackled to life. "Hey there, munchkin," the man who hated everyone practically cooed. "What can your uncle P.P. do for you?"

"Uncle P.P. can call the exterminators," Justice answered in a dry voice. "We have bugs."

Daisy sighed. "Pretorius?"

"Still here."

"Cancel the exterminators. You don't have bugs. You have…well…me."

Justice hunkered down on the floor and peered at the insect. Then he shot her a look that should have fried her on the spot. He spared Noelle a quick glance that told Daisy whom she had to thank for her reprieve. A temporary reprieve, no doubt.

"Are you an alien bug or a domestic one?" Pretorius asked Daisy. "I mean, do I need to worry about you turning into a giant cockroach and eating us, or are you the homegrown garden-variety type of bug that nibbles on leaves and such?"

Daisy's mouth twitched. "And such."

"Then quit bothering me. Jett and I are working on a new program."

Justice climbed to his feet and confronted her with eyes the color of sunshine, yet filled with the coldness of a subzero morning. "What have you done to my house?"

"I improved it. You said I could."

"I do not recall saying you could paint bugs on my wall. Nor do I consider bugs, even virtual ones, an improvement."

She glanced at the floorboard. "I've got news for you, Justice. Anything that covers up all that white is a definite improvement. And actually, it's not a bug. It's a caterpillar."

"Which technically is an insect. That, madam, makes it a bug."

She should have known better than try to outrationalize Mr. Rational, himself. Seizing a different tack, she offered a winning smile. "But a very pretty one, don't you think?"

He pointed at her artwork. "That is the larva of an *actias luna*. Based on its orange shading, I assume it's in its fifth instar." He frowned at the busy little caterpillar. "You do realize that luna moths aren't indigenous to Colorado? It isn't logical. How would it have gotten here?"

Oh, for the love of… Daisy glared at Justice. Enough was enough. "It got here when I painted it on your wall." She spared her daughter another glance. Noelle watched with far too much interest. "Could we discuss this in private? Your office, perhaps?"

"I don't know." He folded gorgeous arms roped with intriguing ripples and bulges across an equally gorgeous chest, also roped with intriguing ripples and bulges. "Are there any insects in there?"

Technically? "No."

"Fine. Come on, Red," he said, using Jett's nickname for his daughter. He scooped her up and settled her into the sling of his crooked arm. "I think we'll both find your mother's explanation highly interesting."

Daisy trailed behind him in the direction of his office. "What part of 'discuss this in private' didn't you understand?" she complained.

"My comprehension continues to be excellent, as I'm sure you're well aware. I simply enjoy having my daughter with me whenever possible."

Daisy released a sigh. How could she argue with that? With increasing regularity she'd catch Justice pausing in his various activities to describe what he was doing to Noelle. For a man who'd so unexpectedly discovered himself in possession of an instant family, he'd sure taken to it like a duck to water. Once she'd even caught him explaining he was about to go to work in his lab, refusing to leave until he'd satisfied himself that Noelle understood his departure was temporary, though Daisy had her doubts about how much their daughter grasped of his technical explanation. Still. It gave her hope for the future.

The instant Justice thrust open the door to his office, his gaze swept the walls. The absence of any *actias lunas* seemed to reassure him, and he relaxed. "Okay, what's going on, Daisy?"

She shrugged. "All the white was getting to me. You gave me permission to make improvements. I made a few."

"As I've already explained, painting bugs on my walls does not improve them." He instantly realized he'd hurt her, that fact reinforced by Noelle's indignant babble. He rubbed his daughter's back in a soothing motion. "You're right, Red. That was thoughtless. I didn't mean it that way. There's no questioning your talent, Daisy. You're a stunning artist."

"But you prefer I confine myself to canvas?" she asked tightly.

A frown creased his brow. "What's wrong, Daisy? What's going on?"

She couldn't bring herself to look at him, to tell him the truth. Instead, she crossed to the window to stare out across a snowy, windswept landscape. White-capped mountains rose in the distance, a fitting backdrop for both the man and his home. "Like I said. All the white around here is making me uncomfortable."

"Funny. I find it reassuring."

Daisy turned and grabbed the opening he'd unwittingly provided. "Why is that, Justice?" At his hesitation, she offered an encouraging smile. "I'm serious. Why is all that white reassuring?"

He gave it a moment's serious thought before replying. Noelle squirmed in his arms and he set her at his feet. Instantly, she tugged at her clothing. No doubt she'd be naked as a jaybird in thirty seconds flat. Or would have if Justice hadn't plucked a child's version of Rumi he'd specifically designed for Noelle from a pile of toys he kept on his desk. He offered it to his daughter. Diverted from her striptease, she plopped down on the floor. After tasting it, her clever little fingers went to work pulling and tugging at the device, delighted when the pieces turned and twisted into different shapes.

Satisfied that she was adequately distracted, Justice shrugged. "I guess I find white reassuring because it stands for possibility," he said. "I spend an inordinate amount of time sitting and thinking."

"Yes, it's part of the creative process."

"No, it's part of the analytical process."

This time she didn't bother to hide her amusement. "Heaven forbid anyone call you creative, huh, Justice?"

"I prefer you not."

"Okay, so staring at a blank wall is part of your analytical process. Would that analytical process be interrupted if the walls were painted?"

"With bugs?"

"Not necessarily. With whatever I wanted to paint."

He speared her with another look, one that struck her as far too perceptive. "I asked you this when we first walked in and I think I should ask again. What's going on, Daisy?"

She didn't want to answer the question. She really didn't.

It cut too close. Hurt too much. Still, he deserved an answer. She tiptoed to within splatter distance of the truth. "I just felt like painting."

He shifted closer, trapping her against his desk. He was so strong. So powerful. So intensely male. And those eyes of his... They glittered with a gold as sharp and brilliant as his intellect. He slid his hand along the sweep of her throat to cup the left side of her face. Unable to resist she turned into the caress, allowed his warmth to seep into her pores and heat her blood. Want stirred, leaving her utterly helpless to resist.

"Talk to me, Daisy," he murmured. "I know you've been keeping something from me. What is it?"

She debated for a long moment. What good did it do to hide the truth? Maybe if she explained, he'd understand. Blowing out a sigh, she closed her eyes and confessed. "That caterpillar? It's the first thing I've painted in a while."

He froze. "Define a while?"

She shrugged. "A longish string of days."

"Longish, as in twenty months, eight days, seventeen hours and twenty-nine minutes?"

She opened her eyes, hoping they didn't reflect the intensity of her misery, and nodded. "To the nanosecond."

Without a word, he drew her into his arms and held her. The delicious scent of him flooded her senses. So did his strength and determination. It was as though by being here with him, she'd absorbed bits and pieces of him. She couldn't explain it, certainly didn't understand it. She could only accept and revel in being with him again and experiencing the return of her creativity, even though she suspected it had a lot to do with the man who held her.

"Perhaps this is the appropriate time to make a confession of my own," he murmured.

"You can't paint, either?"

A chuckle escaped him. "No." His humor faded. "And I also can't work. In my case, it's been going on for longer than twenty months, eight days—"

"—seventeen hours and twenty-nine minutes?"

"Thirty-one," he corrected absently. "And I'd say it's been closer to two years, two months and thirteen days. I can provide you with the hours and minutes if you require."

"That's not necessary. I get the idea. So what happened two years—" Her breath escaped in a rush. "Oh, Justice. Your accident?"

"Yes. That's when I realized that, other than Pretorius, I had no one in my life. At least, no one who would miss me if I were gone."

"And you wanted someone?"

He swept her hair back from her face and smiled at her, something vaguely bittersweet clinging to the corners of his mouth. "Very much."

"No wonder you resorted to a computer program to find a wife." She caught her bottom lip between her teeth. "Instead, you're stuck with me."

"I guess that means we're stuck with each other."

She searched his face for a clue to his innermost feelings. "Are we, Justice?"

"Only if we want to be. And only if we can find a way to make our relationship work. With that in mind, I suggest it's time for another condition."

"Oh, great. One of yours or one of mine?"

"How about one that's ours," he suggested. "Joint Condition One. You have permission to paint on walls. Certain walls and *only* certain walls."

Everything inside softened and warmed. "Really?" she asked, delighted.

"I want this to be your home, too, and if that's what it takes to unblock your artistic talent and get you painting again, I'm more than willing to sacrifice a few white walls."

Daisy wrapped her arms around Justice's waist and hugged him tight. "Thank you. I promise you won't be sorry."

He wrapped her up in a snug embrace. "Before you get too excited, the labs downstairs and all of Pretorius's areas are strictly off-limits." She could feel his steady heartbeat against her cheek, while his voice rumbled in her ear. "You may paint down to the bottom of the steps leading to the basement area, but no farther. Understood?"

"Understood." She tilted back her head and smiled up at him. "You may even discover you like what I've done so much you want me to paint those walls, too."

He swore so softly Jett's behavior modification program didn't catch it. Nor did Noelle, thank goodness. "We're not kids anymore, Daisy. This isn't like the lines I used to draw, lines you took such delight in stepping over."

She had a sneaking suspicion it was exactly like the lines he'd drawn all those years ago, lines meant to box her out. Instead, she'd forced her way in, forced him to expand those lines to include her. Just as she was doing now. But he'd have to discover that for himself. "Thank you, Justice. Thank you for understanding."

"You're welcome." As though unable to resist, he kissed her, the moment one of the sweetest she'd experienced since her arrival. "Well? What are you waiting for? You have walls to paint."

"I'm on it, I'm on it."

Daisy bolted across the office and closed the door behind her. Then she waited. She knew the instant he saw what she'd done to his office wall—the painting of Emo X-14 peeking at him from behind the safety of the door, his electronic control helmet askew, processors twinkling, his row of aquamarine eyes glowing with mischief.

"Son of a—!" *Wheep!*

Daisy grinned. Whether Justice liked it or not, he now had people who cared about him. And with luck it would help him work again. With luck they'd find a way to blend their imperfect little group into the perfect family.

Nine

Perhaps it happened because Justice gave his permission to paint the walls. Perhaps it was because his analytical block mirrored her own creative one. Or perhaps happiness gave her the release she needed, but when Daisy woke the next day, it was with the overwhelming urge to paint. Not just caterpillars, but entire sweeps of lovely, blank wall.

And paint she did.

The floodgates opened and there weren't enough hours in the day to transpose all the ideas rampaging through her head into painted images. Little by little, the house transformed as furnishings arrived and lush jungles exploded to life. Exotic creatures peeked from corners or flitted along the ceiling or whimsically appeared in unexpected places, much to everyone's amusement and delight.

But the section that gave Daisy the most pleasure was the stairway leading to areas off-limits. There she painted an amusing rendition of Noelle creeping down the steps, a mischievous expression on her impish face, the little girl trailed by Kit, Cat and all manner of creatures. At the very bottom of the staircase, one naughty toe crossed over Justice's line and into forbidden territory.

Daisy knew the instant Justice spotted that single, defiant toe. His roar of laughter echoed up the stairwell, the sound so unexpected, so unrestrained and so painfully rare, that it had everyone in the household scurrying to see what had caused his amusement. Even Pretorius made an appearance, though he only stayed long enough to chuckle before darting the group a nervous glance and scampering back to his computer room. He'd actually relented later that day and gave her a brief, nervous tour, no doubt at Jett's insistence. But Daisy knew it was a start.

It gave her hope that they were all coming together as a family, and maybe, just maybe, she and Justice would be able to make a permanent commitment and…as he put it "bond" and "form a family unit." Or as she put it, fall in love. Maybe she'd have taken up permanent residence in her personal fantasyland if she hadn't had a conversation with Cord while working on the final home improvements.

"I'd like to create a better flow between these two rooms, maybe open up this section of wall." Daisy pointed to a long expanse of painful white. "I can't imagine what the architect was thinking to close it off."

"Wasn't the architect. Used to be open," the huge man informed her. "That Pamela woman…beg pardon…*Dr. Randolph*, as she insisted I call her, had it closed up and plastered over. Might have a bunch of fancy initials after her name, but I gotta tell you, Daisy. That woman was an idiot."

Daisy froze, thinking fast. She suspected if she expressed ignorance about Dr. Randolph, Cord would clam up. He was that sort of man. "I didn't realize the wall had been one of her decisions," she said in what she hoped was a casual manner. "I'm surprised Justice didn't have you change it back to the way it was."

"Nope. He was more concerned with getting all her fancy East Coast furniture cleared out right pronto. Never did suit the place. All stiff and formal and cold. Like her, if you know what I mean." His gaze swept the improvements Daisy had made and a satisfied smile settled on his broad, homely face. "Just like I can look at your changes and know what kind of person you are."

"I hope that's a good thing," she murmured.

"Very good." He slanted her a quick, curious look. "You one of his apprentices, too? You don't strike me as the type."

"No," she replied, hoping she didn't sound too forlorn. "I wouldn't qualify. I'm not an engineer." Or anything close.

After Cord left, Daisy thought long and hard about what he'd told her. Justice had never mentioned that he'd actually found an apprentice/wife. Or that it hadn't worked out. While part of her wondered why their relationship ended, another part couldn't contain her relief that it had. How would she have handled it if she'd arrived on Justice's doorstep only to be faced with a Mrs. Dr. St. John? Daisy flinched at the idea.

So, what did she do now? Confront him or keep the knowledge to herself? Pamela's existence and Justice's continued use of the apprentice/wife program hurt, she finally decided. Seriously hurt, even though they weren't together at the time. They would have to discuss it at some point. But not yet. Not when everything and everyone rested on a knife's edge. She'd give them time to grow closer, to see if he wouldn't open up on his own. And then she'd demand answers.

Her assessment proved sound when Aggie decided to throw her first bridge party. "They're just some people I met in town," the housekeeper explained. "Since socializing is difficult with everyone spread out, we decided to meet on a weekly basis to play cards. So, I was wondering…" She clutched her hands together. "Could we meet here?"

"I'm sure Justice won't mind," Daisy said. "Invite them over."

"Right now it's only two other people. But I'm confident we'll find another player before long. We'll play a dummy hand for our fourth until we do."

"I think it's a great idea. You can use the dining room, if you want. Or, better yet, we can set up a table in the great room in front of the fireplace."

Aggie beamed in delight. "That would be the perfect place for a lovely cup of tea, don't you think?"

"I can't imagine a better one," Daisy replied with an answering smile. "Bridge and tea. You can't improve on that."

"No, you can't."

Justice's only objection on the night of the bridge party related to Pretorius. "He's been dealing with a lot of changes these past couple of weeks." He shot a look toward the great room where Aggie's visitors had gathered. "I don't want him pushed too far."

"If it doesn't work out, we'll reconsider," Daisy replied. "Let's give it a try to see what happens."

"My trick, I believe," a voice boomed from the speakers just then.

Justice shot Daisy a look of utter bewilderment. "That sounds like Pretorius."

The two crept closer to the doorway, staring in fascination. Justice stood behind her, so close she could feel the warmth of his body and hear the give-and-take of her breath. The bridge group sat around a table in front of the fireplace, just as she'd suggested. A sparkling tea service perched on a cart closest to Aggie, dainty cups and saucers at the elbows of the three women gathered there. The fourth position at the table remained empty, although a holder full of cards occupied that portion of the table, facing the fireplace.

"This is delicious tea, Aggie," Pretorius continued from on high.

"Thank you, Pretorius. It's an English blend I order off the internet."

"I appreciate your sending Jett down with a tray so I could enjoy it with the rest of you ladies."

"And we appreciate your being our fourth," one of the women said, her laugh carrying a girlish, almost flirtatious ring. "Maybe, when you feel up to it, you'll consider joining us in person."

Dead silence met the offer. Then to Daisy's utter astonishment, Pretorius said, "Maybe I will."

"Are you having any trouble seeing your cards?" another of the ladies asked. "Do you need the holder moved?"

"An inch to the left would help. No, no, Grace. I should have said *my* left. Yes, that's better. The camera was having trouble focusing on that last card."

"He's playing with them," Daisy whispered. Tears gathered in her eyes and she turned, burying her face against Justice's broad chest. "He's actually interacting with people."

"I never thought he'd be able to change," Justice murmured in a husky voice. "You've only been here nineteen days, three hours and five minutes. And look at the difference you've made."

She could hear the emotion ripping apart his words. Pretorius wasn't the only one changing. She could sense the loosening of Justice's tight control, as well, where the events of the past had left a painful smear on his soul and encouraged a man who already tended to distrust emotions to suppress them entirely. Maybe he'd talk to her about Dr. Pamela, take her deeper into his confidence. Daisy could only hope.

Right now she sensed that he was becoming more the man she knew all those years ago. Allowing his heart—on rare occasions—to rule his intellect. Certainly at night he became that person, the intimacy of their lovemaking allowing him to open what he'd always kept so carefully closed and locked, giving them a place to relate…and grow from. Maybe, just maybe in this season of miracles, he'd learn to trust. To open his heart in the brilliance of daylight, as well as the shadow of night.

Maybe, instead of trying to teach a robot to feel, he'd learn how to do that for himself.

"The program's ready," Pretorius announced. "When you're done playing…?"

Ever so gently, Justice threaded Noelle's tiny hands with a thin band, while his daughter sat—for once still and silent—and watched in fascination while he strung a cat's cradle. "I'm not playing. I'm teaching," he corrected. "There now. We've just made a rectangle. Can you say *rectangle,* Noelle?"

She prattled happily and Justice nodded gravely. "Excellent."

"That wasn't *rectangle,*" Pretorius objected. "That was baby babble."

"Oh, and I suppose P.P. isn't baby babble?"

"P.P!" Noelle crowed, twisting around toward Pretorius.

"See? She associates P.P. with me."

"Not something I'd run around admitting to all and sundry," Justice muttered. He bent attentively over the criss-crossing laces entwined around his daughter's fingers and ever so gently restrung them. "And this, Noelle, is a triangle. Say, *triangle.*"

Pretorius snorted at the baby's laughing coos.

"And this…" He pulled gently on two of the strings. "This is a Christmas star for my Christmas baby."

The excited burst of gibberish came precariously close to the word *star* and left both men beaming in pride at her brilliance. But it was her final word that gutted Justice. A sweet, clear baby-voiced "Dada," followed by her holding out her arms imperiously, still entangled in the cat's cradle. He pulled her close and she mashed her face against his in an awkward, openmouthed kiss.

A cascade of emotion flowed through him, the sensory

input overwhelming. His arms tightened around his daughter and he literally inhaled her. The distinctive baby scent, the incredible softness of her warm skin, the silky strawberry-colored curls that brushed his face. The living, breathing essence of her filled him to overflowing and all he could do was hang on and ride the tidal wave of emotion that threatened to swamp him.

He had no idea how long he indulged in the irrational, before finding his way back to a more normal frame of mind. To his relief, Pretorius self-consciously occupied himself with banging away at his computer, giving Justice time to recover. He started to speak, then discovered he needed to clear his throat for some odd reason.

"Next time we'll work on trapezoids and equilateral parallelograms," he informed his daughter gruffly, holding out his hand for her to clutch. "If you work hard you'll have your geometric shapes mastered by Christmas. Eighteen months, tops."

Pretorius did some throat clearing of his own. "Hey. Dada. Can we get down to business? I don't know how much wall space is left to keep Daisy occupied. If you don't want her getting wind of what we're doing, I suggest you shake a leg."

The instant Justice removed the strings from her fingers Noelle began to wriggle, not pleased with the interruption to their game. "Damn it—" A siren sounded a discordant *wheep, wheep*. "*Darn it*—how am I supposed to get a measuring tape around her? She won't stop squirming."

Noelle stilled, grinned, then fluttered her pale green eyes at him. "Damn."

For some reason the siren didn't sound for the baby. Hell, no. Only when *he* slipped up. "I'm beginning to dislike your computer. A lot."

"Darn it, Justice—" *Wheep!* "It's not my computer. It's Jett's. But if you don't stop breaking Condition One, all heck—" *Wheep!* "—is going to break loose. Now, why the hell is it going off when I'm not even swearing?" *Wheep! Wheep!*

Noelle gurgled. "Damn. Hell." Dead silence.

"This is all your fault," the two men said in concert. They paused in their efforts long enough to glare at each other.

"It's not my fault," Pretorius protested. "That juvenile delinquent hacked in again and set up another Condition One Violation program. Every time I delete it, it pops back up."

"I'll give you one day. After that, I take matters into my own hands and I promise you, it won't be pretty."

"I'll speak to her."

They went back to work. All the while, Noelle fidgeted and burbled and jabbered nonstop, thoroughly enjoying the attention, as well as finally being rid of most of her clothes. Justice shook his head in amusement. If he didn't watch her like a hawk, she'd shed her diaper, too.

"Okay, I have the first measurement," Justice announced. "You ready?"

"Set." Pretorius spun his chair around and sent it shooting across the floor toward his computer banks. He jabbed his eyeglasses higher on the bridge of his nose. "And go."

"Height. 74.2936 centimeters."

"Wait, wait. The comparison chart is in inches, not centimeters."

"Who the hell—" *Wheep!* "—uses inches in scientific measurements?"

"A baby comparison chart."

"Well, convert my measurements from metric to imperial."

Pretorius thrust his hands through his hair, standing the graying tufts on end. "Do you know how long it's been since I…? Never mind." Snatching up his calculator, he banged in a series of numbers. "Okay, 29.2494 inches. Go."

"Weight. 9.0356 kilograms. Let me guess. You need it in pounds."

More banging. "Got it, got it. Go."

"Head circumference. 45.5930 centimeters. I might be a smidge off on that one. She won't stop squirming."

"Head circumference—17.95 inches. Entered." He stabbed a button and waited. "Okay. I have no idea whether this is good or bad, so don't kill the messenger. And for the love of Pete, don't break Condition One."

"Just get to it, old man."

"For height, she's in the 65.1 percentile."

Justice lifted his daughter into his arms and cuddled her close. Not that it was really cuddling. More like a sensible, protective hold with maybe a gentle tickle to distract her. "I am taller than average and height is a dominant gene. It's logical to think she received that particular genetic propensity from me. What about head circumference?"

"Seventy-one percentile." Pretorius spun around. "That mean she's gonna be smart?"

Justice swept his hand across his daughter's blaze of curls. "There have been studies done on the correlation between head size and intellect. Though the results aren't definitive, individuals with high IQ scores do tend to have larger than average heads."

"Literally or figuratively?" Pretorius asked dryly.

Justice refrained from responding since he suspected it would set off the siren again. "What about her weight?"

"Darn." *Wheep!*

Noelle clapped her hands. "Damn."

"Now, don't get upset, Justice, but Noelle is only in the 37.6 percentile."

"What? Run it again."

"I have. Three times. Thirty-seven-point-six." He spun around, a frown forming between thick dark brows. "You think Daisy isn't feeding her enough?" he whispered.

"Not deliberately. From what I've observed she's an excellent mother." Justice gave it some thought. "How much would Noelle have to weigh to be in the fiftieth percentile?"

"She'll need to hit 11.4543 kilograms by Christmas."

Justice nodded. "Then we'd better get busy. You have twenty-four hours to research the appropriate dietetic needs for a female infant of eleven months, twenty-five days and calculate how many additional calories it will require for her to achieve her goal weight."

"On it."

"I'll research potential health risks for underweight toddlers and request to see Noelle's medical records."

"Do you think Daisy will allow you access?"

"Allow you access to what?" Daisy asked, stepping into the lab. She spared Pretorius a quick, apologetic smile. "Sorry to trespass, but the computer said Noelle was down here and it's time for her nap." She returned her attention to Justice. "What do you want access to?"

"Noelle's medical records. She's underweight."

Daisy planted her hands on her hips. "She most certainly is not. She's a perfect weight given her bone structure and energy level."

"She's 3.11 grams off plumb," Pretorius offered helpfully.

One look at Daisy's expression had Justice doing some swift backpedaling. "Noelle does possess her mother's fine bone structure. Does the comparison chart take that into consideration?"

Daisy frowned. "Comparison chart? What comparison chart? And what are those black lines on Noelle?" She caught her breath and glared at Justice in disbelief. "Did you paint grid marks on our baby?"

"You painted flora and fauna on my walls," he retorted a shade defensively.

"That was different," she snapped. "They're walls. This is a baby."

"Correct. My marks have a scientific purpose. Yours are merely for decoration." He flinched at the intense hurt that flickered across her expression, hastening to add, "It's very attractive decoration. And you will recall that I have since given you permission to continue with your project. Joint Condition One, remember?"

"Well, I did not give you permission to turn our baby into a scientific experiment. Nor did I give you permission to cover her in grid marks." Daisy crossed to his side and snatched their daughter from his arms. "Is that all she means to you, Justice? Some sort of research project?"

"No, of course not."

Tears glittered in Daisy's eyes and the expression almost killed him. "I thought you were beginning to care. But I guess I was mistaken. Once a scientist, always a scientist?" With that, she turned on her heel and stalked toward the door.

"Damn, hell," Noelle cooed in farewell, waving her little hands as they exited the room.

"You said it," Justice muttered.

Pretorius released a slow breath. "What now?"

"Now we create our own comparison chart, taking into consideration a few more factors, such as bone structure."

"I can help with that," came a voice from on high.

The two men jumped and the computer let out a shrill *wheep, wheep!* Jett grinned down at them from where she sat curled up on top of the bookcase.

"Now that damn—" *Wheep!* "—siren is going off when I'm even thinking about swearing," Justice growled.

"Weren't you paying attention? It was going off even when we *didn't* swear."

"That was just me." She grinned and waggled a remote at them. "So, what do you say, Uncle P.? Want some help with that program? I'm not doing anything."

"Actually, I believe you're spying on us. Again. And…and *wheeping* us."

"True. But I can do all that while I help. I'm great at multitasking." She leaped nimbly from the bookcase to one of the long counters to the floor. "What are you planning to do if the program still shows Noelle's underweight even after you've altered the parameters?"

"Feed her," the two men said in unison.

"Can't have Justice's daughter off plumb," Pretorius muttered. He kicked a chair in Jett's direction. "Don't just stand there. We have work to do."

Justice didn't delay further, but went after Daisy and his daughter, knowing full well he had some serious groveling to do. He found Daisy in the bathroom, giving Noelle a bath.

"I'm sorry."

It seemed the safest thing to say. Of course, it helped that he meant it with the utmost sincerity. He hadn't intended to hurt her feelings, any more than he intended to treat their daughter like a scientific experiment. Well, not exactly. Daisy kept her back to him, gently rinsing away the water soluble lines crisscrossing Noelle.

"Do you resent my painting on your walls?" she asked, not pretending to misunderstand the apology.

"I did at first," he admitted. "I'm quite partial to white."

"I've noticed."

"But in the last few days I've noticed something odd."

"Something off plumb?" she asked dryly.

"Yes. Quite off plumb, at least for me."

He leaned against the doorjamb and watched her clever hands stroke the marks from Noelle's body. Daisy really did have lovely hands, both gentle and firm, graceful and tantalizing. More than anything he wanted her running those supple fingers over him, teasing and stroking as they chased a path across his body. Gripping him tight while he drove her to climax. Soothing him in that timeless aftermath. He closed his eyes in disbelief. Dear God, it was happening again. All he had to do was look at her and he lost all control. How was that possible?

Daisy shot him a questioning glance over her shoulder.

Fortunately, she didn't seem to notice anything amiss. "What have you noticed, Justice?" she prompted.

He forced himself to focus on the subject at hand. "Each day I find myself searching for any new changes or additions you might have added to the walls. On average I expend a minimum of forty-nine minutes a day on the activity."

Her shoulders tightened and her spine formed a rigid line. "Expend or waste?" she asked crisply.

He debated whether to give her an honest answer and decided he'd never been comfortable lying. With Daisy he found it almost impossible. "At first, I categorized it as a waste. One time I utilized in excess of one hundred and thirty-two minutes attempting to locate all the additions. I'm afraid I can't be more accurate since I—" He cleared his throat. "I lost track of time."

"You, Justice?" Was that a hint of irony he caught?

"I recognize that it's a serious anomaly, but..." He frowned. "I no longer consider it a waste of time."

"Really? You astonish me. Why is that?"

He took her comment at face value. "I've recently discovered the pursuit causes a positive sensory experience that's engaged me outside the realm of my scientific endeavors and altered the manner in which I prioritize various aspects of my life."

"Uh-huh." She lifted a wildly kicking Noelle from the tub and wrapped their daughter up in a fluffy yellow towel that contrasted quite delightfully with her bright strawberry-blond hair. He grinned. They really did have an adorable daughter. "Translation, please?" Daisy requested.

"It...it makes me happy."

Soft color suffused her face and she smiled. Hell, she beamed. "Really? My paintings make you happy?"

"They certainly cause a strong visceral reaction."

"That's one of the sweetest thing you've ever said to me."

He eyed her uncertainly. "Is that sarcasm?"

She carefully set their daughter on the floor, still wrapped in the bath towel. Approaching, she slid her arms around his neck and lifted her face to his. "It's Noelle's nap time. Why don't we put her down and then I'll show you exactly what I'm feeling. I'll even give you a hint." Her laughter sparkled up at him. "It's not sarcasm."

The next hour was one of the most enjoyable he'd ever spent in the middle of a workday. What was it about Daisy that she could so easily divert him? How was she able to decimate rational thought and rock-solid intent with one mischievous glance? And how could he have ever imagined he'd be satisfied with an apprentice/wife programmed to order? The one time he'd attempted it had proven to be an unmitigated disaster. He'd been bored to tears within twenty-four hours. Hell, he'd been bored to tears within twenty-two hours, fourteen minutes and fifty-one seconds.

But not with Daisy. Never with Daisy.

She rolled over and traced the contours of his face, tripped along the taut lines of his jaw. "That was amazing. But then, it always is." She rested her chin on his chest. "Why is that, do you suppose?"

"We're sexually compatible."

She released her breath in a sigh, warning that he hadn't given her the answer she'd hoped. Desperate for a hint, he asked, "Why do you think we're amazing together?"

"I guess there's some truth to that old adage opposites attract."

"It's more than an old adage, it's a scientific fact. At least, when it comes to magnetic properties and electrically charged particles." She laughed, but he caught a hint of wistfulness beneath the humor. "What's wrong, Daisy?"

She drew lazy circles across his chest, painting him with her fingertips. He couldn't help but wonder what colors she was imagining. Dark, passionless ones that glittered with the iciness of a dark winter? Or brilliant shades of springtime hope? "What do you want from our relationship, Justice?"

He wasn't stupid. He could see a trap when it yawned in front of him. He chose his words with extreme care. "I want marriage. I want a family."

"Yes, you explained that was your game plan when I first told you about Noelle. When you told me about your apprentice/wife program," she added with far too casual an air.

His gaze sharpened. "Nothing has changed since then."

"Funny. I'd say a lot has changed since then."

He stirred, uncomfortable with the direction of their conversation. "I meant, nothing about my game plan has changed. I still want marriage. I still want a family. I'm hoping, given time, that our relationship will progress in that direction."

"Like you were hoping it would with Pamela?"

The words hung in the afternoon air. Justice scrubbed his hands across his face and swore. Damn, damn, damn. He'd suspected something was up. Now she'd confirmed it. "I assume Cord told you?"

"You should have been the one to tell me." Then she let him off the hook. Somewhat. "Why don't you tell me now?"

Okay, fair enough. "She seemed like the best candidate for the job." He shrugged. "I was wrong."

"Why didn't you tell me about her when we first arrived?"

"We had enough to deal with. Plus, the relationship didn't work out, so it was no longer an issue."

"Why didn't it work out?"

"Damn it, Daisy. Do you need every last detail?"

She tilted her head to one side in consideration. "Yes."

"Fine." He considered carefully before speaking. "You know what we were saying about opposites attracting? Well, like objects don't. Pamela was too much like me. Hell, she was worse than me. She was logical and rational and brilliant."

"Beautiful, an engineer, kind, someone who won't make waves and who is able to handle the isolation of life in Nowhere, Colorado?"

"Apparently, Cord isn't the only one with a big mouth." When Daisy didn't answer, Justice blew out a sigh. "Yes, she met every single one of my criteria. Are you satisfied now?"

"Not really."

"She met every single one of my criteria, particularly the one about being in control of her emotions. In fact, I've never met a colder, more emotionless woman." He shuddered at the memory. "I have a feeling if I'd ever worked up the nerve to touch her, I'd have died from frostbite."

Daisy couldn't hide her smile. "Then what *do* you require in a wife?"

Damn it to hell. Why did women ask such impossible questions? Why did women get a man naked and in bed, wait until he was at his most vulnerable and incapable of escape, and then blindside him with questions guaranteed to initiate an argument. Okay, he knew why. They were women. Still…

"I want you," he said, hoping it would make a difference. "And although neither of us planned it, I couldn't ask for a better daughter than Noelle."

"Want." She tried out the word. It must not have been the flavor she'd hoped because she discarded it with a tiny wrinkle of her nose. "What about love?"

He closed his eyes and silently swore. He should have seen that one coming, especially with a woman like Daisy. "Is it one of your prerequisites to marriage?" he asked carefully.

"Yes."

He nodded, not surprised. "I wish I had it to offer." He cupped her face, locking gazes with her so she could read his sincerity. "Someone like you deserves love, deserves a husband capable of love. If we decide to marry, you need to know that I can't provide you with that."

Her lashes flickered downward to conceal her eyes, but not

before he saw the sheen of tears. "What *are* you offering?" she whispered.

She was killing him by inches, but he forced himself to be brutally honest. "I'll give you everything I have. My home. My intellect. My money. Sex." His mouth twisted in a parody of a smile. "According to you, amazing sex. I've even given you my walls. But I can't give you what I don't possess."

"And you don't think you possess the capacity to love?"

"No, Daisy. I don't think it," he stated ever so gently. "I know I don't."

He was going to lose her.

Justice woke to the knowledge while dawn's first light invaded Daisy's bedroom. His hold on her tightened convulsively and she stirred in her sleep, murmuring in protest. He didn't doubt for one tiny second that she was going to leave him and he fought a growing sense of panic as the certainty became stronger with each passing moment. He had to do something, anything, to keep her. Unfortunately, the three simple words guaranteed to make her his, were the only three he couldn't in all good conscience utter.

The irony didn't escape him. He'd always thought he possessed everything a woman could possibly want. He was worth billions. Owned a company respected around the world. Boasted a respectable intellect. Even better, he wanted marriage. A family. He frowned in bewilderment. Most women would be satisfied with that, wouldn't they?

Unfortunately, Daisy wasn't "most women." Rather than reveling at the idea of spending his money, she'd used a mere pittance of his billions. And for what? To transform his house into a home. She'd only made one serious demand of him, regardless of her ridiculous conditions—that he involve himself in their daughter's life. And wouldn't he have done everything within his power, given all that he possessed to be allowed that opportunity, even if she hadn't insisted? The only real request she'd made on her own behalf had been to paint his walls. And what had she done when he'd reluctantly agreed? Created magnificent murals that stunned the senses and delighted the eye.

With each passing minute, light eclipsed darkness, marching relentlessly across the mattress. It encompassed Daisy within a halo of radiance and yearning, pouring passion onto passion while he remained caught within night's lingering death. Gently, tenderly, he slipped from her embrace, and withdrew from the light and warmth aboveground to retreat to the darkness below.

No, there wasn't any question. Daisy was going to leave and he had to do something, find a way—any way that didn't involve lying to her—to convince her to stay.

She couldn't stay.

Daisy woke to the knowledge while dawn's first light streamed into her bedroom. Beside her, Justice's hold tightened protectively and she stirred against him, murmuring a reassurance. She didn't doubt for one tiny second the need to leave and she fought a growing sense of panic as the certainty became stronger with each passing moment. She would do almost anything if it meant she didn't have to go. Unfortunately, three simple words stood between them, creating a gulf that couldn't be bridged.

The irony didn't escape her. Justice possessed everything a woman could possibly want. He was worth billions. Owned a company respected around the world. Boasted a respectable intellect. Even better, he wanted marriage. A family. She struggled against tears. Most woman would be satisfied with that, wouldn't they?

Why couldn't she be like "most women"? Why couldn't she be satisfied with the material possessions he had to offer, the physical relationship that bordered on incandescent, the heart-wrenching way he'd taken to fatherhood? He loved, even if he didn't believe it. She saw it every time he looked at his daughter. But did he love her? Were the words that important? She closed her eyes and faced the painful truth. Without those words—and the emotions behind them—the rest held no real meaning. Not for her. She'd trade all the other trappings in a heartbeat if only Justice loved her.

With each passing minute, light eclipsed darkness, slipping effortlessly across the mattress. It encompassed her within a halo of radiance and yearning, pouring passion onto passion while Justice remained caught within night's lingering death. Gently, with unmistakable finality, he slipped from her embrace, and withdrew from the light and warmth aboveground to retreat to the darkness below.

No, there wasn't any question. She was going to have to leave, even though everything within her cried out to stay.

Ten

Daisy started to enter Justice's lab and hesitated at the sound of Noelle's voice. "Wuv you," she demanded, patting her father's cheek, her lashes fluttering flirtatiously.

"Yes, I love you very much," Justice assured her as he made an adjustment to Emo's helmet. The instant he finished, he leaned over and kissed his daughter, and Daisy caught the sheer, unadulterated love in his gaze when Noelle grabbed his ears and pulled him in for a second helping.

A worried frown darkened her brow. "Emo wuv you?"

"Yes, Emo loves you, too."

He grinned at the exuberant hug and kiss Noelle gave the X-14 model. "Now why is he your favorite? And don't try to tell me he isn't because I'd be forced to call you a teeny-tiny fibber." Noelle babbled in reply and he listened seriously. "Yes, maybe 15 is a bit too sleek, but then he is an upgrade." More babble and more serious consideration. "Huh. I hadn't considered painting the chassis. No doubt your mommy could design something bright and colorful, probably paint whimsical faces on them to give them personality. Hmm. Now that I think about it, that's not a bad idea."

Noelle babbled away, this time at Emo, and to Daisy's amusement, Emo emitted a series of beeps and hums that only served to encourage their daughter's efforts to communicate. She waved her hands, her piquant features scrunched into an intensely focused frown while she chattered away in her own private baby language. All the while, Justice watched and listened, his focus equally intense, as though attempting to decipher her meaning.

When the words wound down, he scooped Noelle into his arms and cradled her against his heart. She curled up there with a happy sigh and he closed his eyes, such an expression of undisguised love on his face, it was painful to witness. Daisy stared down at the stack of papers she held, blinking back tears. How could he believe himself incapable of love? How could he doubt it for even one tiny nanosecond? And how could she get him to see the truth?

Aggie appeared in the hallway just then and tossed a quick smile in Daisy's direction before hurrying into the lab. Daisy followed behind, relieved that the interruption gave her a moment to regain control of her emotions. "It's time for Noelle's lunch," the housekeeper announced. "Would you like me to bring her back down here after her nap?"

"If you wouldn't mind." Justice reluctantly handed over the baby and turned his attention to Daisy. "Perfect timing. I have an idea I want to run by you."

"Giving Emo a paint job?" she guessed.

He stared in surprise. "How did you know?"

"I overheard you discussing it with Noelle." Before she could ask him about the papers she held—the reason for her visit—she was distracted by endless images of herself cycling across the computer screens around the room. "Good Lord. What are these pictures for?"

"They're photos of your emotional responses to various

stimuli. I have videos, too." He lifted a sooty eyebrow. "You may recall I did ask."

The memory clicked. They'd been right here in his lab, the day he'd first introduced her to Emo. "Oh, right. You want to teach Emo to read our expressions." For some reason all those photos made her uncomfortable, perhaps because they showed her expressing such a range of emotions, some of them downright painful. "You have videos, too?"

"Yes. They're excellent teaching tools."

"Can you show me?"

Justice picked up a remote control and aimed it at one of the computers. Instantly, the screen switched from slide show to video and exhibited an image of her walking toward the kitchen. She remembered that day. It had been weeks ago, not long after she'd arrived and before she'd begun to paint the walls. It had been an unusually bad afternoon and she watched in dismay, forced to relive her misery.

The camera switched angles, revealing Aggie puttering at the kitchen table, chopping vegetables for a salad. At the sound of the door opening, she glanced up, a hint of concern drifting across her expression. Daisy dragged herself to the table, took a seat beside the housekeeper and buried her head in her arms.

"I gather the painting didn't go well?" Aggie asked sympathetically. She reached out, her hand skimming across Daisy's head in a motherly caress.

"You could say that." Daisy lifted her face, her expression miserable. "I don't understand, Aggie. I should be over it by now. But every time I see that blank canvas…" The breath shuddered from her lungs and her voice escaped, low and desperate. "I don't think I'll ever paint again."

Aggie tutted, worry pulling at the lines bracketing her mouth. "Of course you will. It's only a matter of when," she said, her encouraging comment ripe with sympathy.

"How long a when, Aggie? It's been nearly two years. It's

like the desire to paint has drained right out of me. I lost it right after Justice and I…" She trailed off and shook her head. "Anyway, I thought maybe I'd find it here."

For an instant Aggie appeared at a loss, then she said bracingly, "Now that you're with Justice again, I'm betting it'll come storming back. You wait and see."

"I love…" Tears filled her eyes and she shook her head, the words bottling in her throat.

Daisy remembered she'd been about to admit she loved Justice, that her hopelessness on that front had infected her creative ability, and had ever since they'd parted nearly two years before. But she'd been unable—or unwilling—to admit the painful truth and had altered what she'd ultimately said. She slid a sideways look at Justice. Did he know? Had he picked up on the subtext at all?

"I love painting so much," the video continued, her true feelings for Justice left unstated. "You have no idea how much I miss it."

"There, there, sweetheart. You've gone and gotten yourself all upset." Setting aside her vegetable peeler, Aggie bustled to the stove and turned on the burner beneath a copper kettle. "How about a nice cup of tea to cheer you up?"

"Thanks, Aggie." Daisy forced out a smile. "I don't know what I'd do without you and your tea. I'm feeling better already."

The clip ended and Daisy fought against that old sense of panic and fear and helplessness. Before she could say anything, Justice was there. He tugged the papers from her hand, tossed them aside and pulled her tight into his arms.

"I'm sorry. In all honesty, I'd forgotten that particular video was the next one in the queue. That was thoughtless of me. There are times I think I could use the sort of emotion chip I'm attempting to design for Emo." He held her, offering his strength and compassion, while she struggled to regain some distance from the events he'd taped. "Are you all right?"

"I'll survive." She pulled back, determined to stand on her own. "I don't understand. Why would you keep that video, Justice, when you must know how painful it is?"

"Precisely because it is so emotional. You four are rarely sad. I have several of Noelle crying, but it's not quite the same. Adults aren't as open as children. I want Emo capable of spotting more subtle cues."

"That was hardly subtle," she pointed out.

"True. I thought if I started with more obvious emotions, we could refine his program over time." He picked up the remote. "I can delete it if you prefer. I have other videos of Jett, Pretorius and Aggie. Granted, none of them are sad, but they cover a sufficient emotional range."

That stopped her. "Jett, Pretorius and Aggie. And me." She shot him an odd look. "What about you, Justice? Do you also have teaching videos of your emotional range?"

A muscle jerked in his jaw. "No."

"Is that because you aren't expressive?" She paused a beat, her heart aching for him. "Or is it because you don't believe you experience those emotions?"

He flinched. It was barely perceptible, but it was there. And she caught it. "I experience certain emotions. Just none that will benefit Emo." Pain filled his gaze and she knew beyond a shadow of a doubt he wasn't talking about sharing his emotions with the robot, but about sharing them with her. "I can't give Emo what I don't possess."

"You're wrong, Justice," she dared to argue. "You do possess those emotions. Granted, you've safeguarded them behind locked doors and thrown away the key. But if you'd just let me in—"

"What if you discover there's nothing behind the locked doors?" he cut in. "That I'm emotionless. Lacking in empathy."

Her eyes narrowed. "You're quoting someone. Who?"

He shrugged. "Any number of foster parents and counselors. Hell, even my own mother and father never understood me."

"Oh, Justice. You were a ten-year-old child when they died. I'm sure that's not true."

He simply stared at her, his glorious eyes blank and empty of all expression. "You're wrong. I overheard my mother say just that, not long before her death. She was talking to my father about me. She said she thought I was incapable of love. That I took after Pretorius and would turn out just like him."

Daisy's mouth dropped open. "You're not incapable of love, any more than Pretorius is," she retorted fiercely. "He may have a social anxiety disorder, but he's one of the most caring, loving people I've ever met. And damn it, so are you. Is that why you refuse to say the words? Because someone was foolish enough to believe you incapable of love and you bought into their ridiculous assumptions?"

"Enough." He stepped away, turning his back on her. "Why are you here, Daisy?"

She debated pressing the issue. But the coldness in his voice, along with the stiffness of his stance warned of the futility of making the attempt. Instead, her gaze settled on the stack of papers he'd tossed aside. A timely reminder. She crossed to his workbench and fanned through the pages before tidying the stack.

"Justice, are you still looking for an apprentice/wife?"

"No. After Pamela…" He shrugged. "The program needs further modification. Besides, I no longer have any use for an apprentice. In a few years Noelle will fill that role nicely. Now I'm just interested in acquiring a wife."

The matter-of-fact statement nearly brought her to her knees. She opened her mouth to say something, anything, but couldn't get the words past the knot in her throat. She shoved the stack of papers in his direction. "You're interested in acquiring one of these women for your future wife?" she managed to ask.

Puzzled, he picked up the first several pages and scanned them. "These are from my apprentice/wife program. How did you get hold of them?"

"The printer was spitting out women when I walked past."

"Huh. I guess the program is still running."

"I read the bios on these women. I'm nothing like them, am I, Justice?"

"No. You're nothing like these women." He flipped through a few pages. "This one has a PhD in Biological Systems Engineering. Useless to me as an apprentice. This next one appears perfect on paper, but so did Pamela. Besides, she looks mean." He showed her the photo. "Doesn't she look mean to you? This one's got *city girl* written all over her. This next one with the glasses has a crazed look about the eyes. No, none of them fit my parameters."

"Your parameters for the perfect wife." When he didn't immediately reply, she added, "These women aren't perfect, Justice. No one is. There's no such thing."

"I know that."

"Do you?" She stepped closer, fixing her gaze on him. "Why do you want me, Justice? Is it because I'm Noelle's mother or because I'm me? I'm not just a body, you know, not just someone to warm your bed." She gestured in the direction of the printouts. "Nor am I a list of parameters some program has spit out. I'm *me,* damn it. And my list of parameters for the right husband—not the perfect husband, but the *right* husband—includes an emotional connection."

He closed his eyes. "We discussed this. I explained—"

"Why are you building a robot that can interpret emotions? Is it so Emo can tell you what you can't figure out for yourself…how people feel? How many versions of Emo have there been? How many Emos have been dismantled and their parts repurposed?" She hammered the questions at him. "Is that what's going to happen to me if you're dissatisfied with the way I function? When you realize you can't mold me into your idea of perfection? I'll be scrapped so you can start over?"

If she'd hoped for an emotional reaction, she finally got one. "Have I ever said any of those things to you?" he demanded. "Have I ever demanded perfection from you?"

"Not exactly."

Fierce anger glittered to life, turning his tawny gaze from cool and remote to incandescent. "Oh, please. Please do be exact. And allow me to repeat… Have I ever said anything along those lines?"

"No," she grudgingly admitted.

"No." The satisfaction sweeping through that single word set her teeth on edge. "I've never said it. And, for your information, I've never even thought it."

"You must have at some point," she snapped back. "Since I have a mile-high stack of women specifically tailored for the role of Mrs. Sinjin, Incorporated, all somewhat short of perfect because you haven't fine-tuned the program."

"If I'd wanted one of those women in that stack, she'd be here right now instead of you. I'd have chosen Pamela. Or I would have picked someone at that engineering conference twenty months, twenty-five days, twenty…twenty—" He heaved the remote against the wall where it shattered. "Damn it to *hell,* Daisy! I can't even tell you the hours and minutes, you have me so pissed off with your endless pushing, pushing, pushing."

She stared, stunned. "Twenty-one hours and twelve minutes ago," she whispered.

He closed his eyes, exhaustion carving deep lines alongside his mouth. "Let me make myself perfectly clear. The only woman I want is you."

That simple statement had the anger draining right out of her. She went to him, wrapped herself up in him. His arms closed around her, pulling her tight. "What are we going to do, Justice?"

"Keep trying. We have to keep trying." He lifted her face to his, took her mouth in an endless kiss. "Please, Daisy. Please, don't give up on me."

But she did. He discovered that painful fact the very next day.

"Phone call from Cord O'Malley," the computer announced.

"Put him through," Justice ordered. He waited until the computer made the connection, before asking, "Yes, Cord, what can I do for you?"

"I just wanted to confirm a work order."

Impatient with the interruption, Justice returned his focus to Emo and settled his magnifying headset over his face. "Daisy is in charge of all work orders. I thought I made that clear."

"You did. But since you're the one paying the bills, I thought I'd better check before we hopped on this particular job."

"Fine. What does the job entail? More furniture? Plumbing or electrical alterations?" He touched the tip of his tool to one of Emo's circuits and a brief smile slipped across his mouth. "Or maybe she's run out of walls to paint and wants you to add a few."

"Actually, this does have to do with painting walls. Only she wants me doing the painting."

"Don't be ridiculous," Justice responded absently. "They're already painted."

"Yeah, that's the thing. I thought those pictures she drew were real pretty, but she wants us to whitewash over them. And take out all that nice furniture she bought. Even the Christmas tree. Strip it post-Pamela clean. Her exact words."

Justice's attention snapped to the conversation with laser-sharp focus. Straightening, he yanked off his headset and tossed it to his workbench. "What the hell are you talking about?" He bit out the words.

The sound of a hand slapping paper came through the speakers. "I'm talking about this work order I have right here that says I'm supposed to come the day after Christmas and yank out all that furniture we dragged in there and paint every last wall white. I'm talking about this work order that says we're supposed to... Hang on and I'll read it like she wrote it. We're to, quote, return the house to the exact same condition it was before our advent. Strip it post-Pamela clean. End quote. Now unless my dictionary is mistaken, that means put everything back the way it was before she came."

Justice fought to breathe. "Your dictionary isn't mistaken, but the work order is. You will ignore it. Is that clear?"

"She's put an after-Christmas rush on it."

"I'm canceling the rush. I will, of course, send you a cancellation fee for your trouble."

"Aw, Justice, you know that's not necessary. I figured there had to be some sort of mistake. I gotta tell you, I'm glad to get it cleared up. I think I'd've cried like a baby if she made me paint those walls."

"Agreed. Please check with me if any further work orders are issued."

"Will do. Hope you have a Merry Christmas."

But Justice wouldn't have a Christmas, merry or otherwise. Not if Daisy left. Not if she took his daughter with her. He couldn't bear the thought of Aggie and Jett leaving, either. They'd become too important to him. Vital to his happiness and well-being. Just as he was willing to bet he and Pretorius had become vital to their happiness. They were a family, damn it, and no matter what it took, he had to find a way to stop her. To convince her to stay. To convince her that they belonged together. All of them.

For the next three days, as the calendar crept steadily closer to Christmas, Justice vacillated between confronting

Daisy over the work order and waiting until after the twenty-fifth. Concern that a confrontation might convince her to leave before the holiday was all that kept him silent. During the day he worked like a man possessed, hoping that even if he couldn't love, maybe his robot's ability to sense emotion would help him analyze the problem and come up with a logical solution. And with each passing night their lovemaking took on an element of desperation, as though they both sensed their time together would soon end.

On Christmas Eve she slipped from his bed and returned to her own room, and he knew he'd lost. Silently, he paced through the house, picturing it without the noise and laughter and joy that had permeated each and every room since Daisy and her household had arrived.

He paused in front of the Christmas tree, one they'd all decorated together. It had been Pretorius's first visit above stairs. Justice tapped an ornament, a miniature laptop with ho-ho-ho scrawled across the tiny screen. Pretorius had given it to Jett to symbolize the bond the two of them had cemented. And he'd given Daisy one of a cradle with Baby's First Christmas inscribed on it.

Finally, he returned downstairs to the lab. He still had a few more hours in which to complete the Emo X-15 model and he intended to use each and every precious minute remaining to him in the hope that he'd finally succeed at getting the upgrade fully operational. He booted up the computer and accessed the list of "emotion" files Pretorius had put together. His uncle had labeled one of them Love, and Justice couldn't remember ever viewing those.

There were still photos as well as videos and he clicked on them at random. The first were a series of Daisy and Noelle and he smiled at the stream of images. Blowing kisses. Snuggling. Bath time. Story time. Bedtime. There were even a few of Jett, curled up with Noelle like a pair of exhausted kittens.

And then he hit an endless cascade of photos of himself with his daughter and his breath stopped. They were pictures he hadn't even known existed, and as he scrutinized one after another he couldn't mistake the look on his face, any more than he'd been able to mistake it on Daisy's.

But it was the final photo that threatened to utterly destroy him. He'd just come from the outside and was still in his coat while he held his sleeping daughter in his arms, his embrace as gentle as it was protective. But he wasn't looking at his daughter in this photo. He was looking at Daisy, who busily painted a picture of Emo, oblivious beneath his watchful gaze. And there, written in his own face, he saw the truth.

He saw love.

Who the hell had he been fooling? All this time he'd been using science and logic as a buffer, refusing to see what was right in front of his eyes. Afraid to take that leap of faith in case he found empty air beneath his feet instead of solid ground. But here he stood, rooted by what he saw. There in stark relief was an undeniable love, from the small, tender way his mouth curved, to the adoring gleam in his eyes, to the hunger written into every line and crevice of his face.

He loved her.

He shot to his feet, intent on telling her just that, but froze at the last moment. Would she believe him? Or would she think it was desperation speaking, a last-ditch effort to convince her to stay. How the hell could he hope to prove to her that he genuinely loved her, especially considering how slow he'd been figuring it out?

There was only one possible way. He needed proof. He needed… His attention shifted to Emo X-15's sleek form. He needed a robot capable of detecting emotion. "There's a chance. There's still a chance," he muttered.

"Where's Justice?" Jett whispered to Pretorius, though Daisy overheard. Overheard and could have wept.

"Where he always is these days," Pretorius answered glumly. "In his lab."

"But it's Christmas. Even you're up here."

Pretorius shrugged uneasily and straightened the bow on one of the presents before tucking it under the gaily lit tree. Instantly, Kit pounced on it, and proceeded to shred the bow. "Maybe he's forgotten. We never did a full-blown Christmas before. It could have slipped his mind."

"Maybe someone should remind him," Jett replied and pulled a remote control from her pocket. With a casual air, she fiddled with the buttons.

Daisy snatched a deep breath. Enough was enough. She'd hoped having Cord call about the work order would give Justice the nudge he needed. That facing the loss of all the improvements she'd made over the past month would be sufficient to force him to his senses. She should have known better. He'd always been in full possession of his senses. Which could only mean one thing.

Clearly she'd misjudged him. Misjudged what he wanted. Misjudged his intentions. Misjudged how he felt. That he could somehow come to love her.

"Okay, everyone," she said with a determined smile. "Time to open presents."

Justice didn't remember how long he worked into the night. Until three? Four? A determined *wheep! wheep!* woke him from a sound sleep. Damn Jett and that blasted…

He shot to his feet, looking around in confusion. What? When? Where? For the second time in recent memory his inner clock failed him. "Computer, date and time?" he demanded in a rusty voice.

"December twenty-fifth, 11:02:12 a.m.," came the dispassionate response.

He swore, then thrust his hands through his hair in an attempt to comb it into some semblance of neatness. Not that it helped. Between the beginnings of the sandpaper beard shadowing his jaw, eyes he didn't doubt were rimmed in sleepless red, and wrinkles pressed into his face from conking out at his workbench, he looked like someone who'd been ridden hard and put away wet.

He glanced at the robot and groaned. He'd tried. He'd worked so long and hard, worked like a maniac, in flat-out desperation. It hadn't changed a damn thing. Emo X-15 still didn't work, any more than its predecessor. He'd failed. Sinking into his chair, he scrubbed his hands across his face. He was so tired. So drained. For the first time in his life he was at a loss, uncertain how or where to move from here, longing for something he couldn't name. Didn't dare name. And yet, the names came to him, anyway.

Daisy. Noelle. Even Aggie and Jett had become part of his life. Part of what made his house a home. And he'd blown it. Failed at every turn.

"You look tired," a cool, remote voice announced.

Justice froze. Slowly he looked up. X-15 hummed with electronic life. "What did you say?"

"You look tired," X-15 repeated.

"Would you like a cup of tea?" came another hesitant voice, the voice of a robot he should have repurposed long ago... and hadn't had the heart to.

Maybe he'd kept it because Noelle adored the older robot. Maybe it was because of Daisy's softhearted attitude toward it. Or maybe it was his own reluctant affection for the silly thing. He fought for control, struggled to remain calm and rational. "Why are you asking me that question?" he asked X-14.

Emo emitted a tiny, nervous beep, as though afraid it had done something wrong. Then it spoke. "You feel sad. Tea will make you feel better."

And that's when he saw his two choices stretching before him. On one hand, the cold logic that had been his close companion for most of his life. On the other, sheer emotion.

And he smiled as he reached for Emo. For the *perfect* Emo. Because he'd just discovered an amazing truth.

Logic wouldn't get him a cup of tea.

Justice raced up the stairs, his hastily wrapped Christmas gifts overflowing his arms. He hit the top step at the same moment Daisy announced, "Okay, everyone. Time to open presents."

"Hang on," he called. "I have a few more to put under the tree." He stepped into the great room and caught Daisy's expression, a heartbreaking gaze full of pain and hope. "Sorry to keep everyone waiting. I was putting the finishing touches on my gifts."

"What did you get me?" Jett demanded greedily.

He selected hers and placed the remaining packages under the tree, rescuing them from Kit's eager claws. "This is a joint gift from Pretorius and me."

Jett ripped open the long, narrow box without hesitation and peered inside. Papers were nestled beneath tissue paper. She used more caution now, lifting them out and carefully unfolding them. Her breath caught. "These…these are letters of recommendation."

"For college," Justice confirmed.

She clutched them to her chest. "From The. Great. Justice. St. John."

"And from me," Pretorius groused. "I'm not exactly chopped liver, you know. It so happens I'm a highly respected member of the computer community."

"Thanks, Uncle P."

She raced to his side and gave him an exuberant hug, one that should have sent him into an immediate panic. Instead he turned a deep shade of red and patted her awkwardly on her back. "Now, now. That's quite enough of the mushy stuff. You haven't even seen the real present."

"There's more?"

She pulled free of the embrace and gently refolded the letters of recommendation as though they were made of spun gold before opening the envelope that accompanied them. She read the note inside, her face crumpling.

"Jett?" Daisy asked uneasily.

"It's…it's a full scholarship, all expenses paid, from Sinjin, Incorporated for the college of my choice, anywhere in the world." She buried her face in her hands.

"Of course, you have to get accepted first," Justice warned.

This time she flew into his arms and wrapped him up in a tight, teary hug. "Thank you. You couldn't have given me a better present."

"Well, now," Aggie said, dabbing at her eyes. "I do believe this calls for a nice cup of tea."

Pretorius selected another gift from under the tree, a large square box, and offered it to the housekeeper. "In that case, you'll need this."

Unlike Jett, Aggie opened her present with care, removing the ribbons and sliding a fingernail beneath the tape. Neatly unfolding the wrapping paper, she set it aside "to add to my scrapbook." Finally, she lifted the top from the box. "Oh, Pretorius. You couldn't have picked a better gift." She eased the dainty teapot from its protective paper. "It's Spode, isn't it?"

"Their Christmas tea set," he confirmed. "And Justice is giving you a selection of teas from around the world. You'll get a new one every week."

She gave the men a misty smile. "Well, then, we'll just have to try out a lovely cup of tea in my new teapot, won't we?"

Jett emerged from beneath the tree, carrying one of Justice's haphazardly wrapped presents. "I found this for Noelle." She handed it to the toddler and helped with the wrapping paper. "Check it out! It's a baby Emo. Does it work any better than the other ones?"

"Nowhere near as well," he admitted with a sly grin, then gestured toward the tree. "Any more presents under there?"

"Something for you," Daisy announced. She handed him a large, sketch pad-size gift, as well as an envelope. "I suggest you start with the envelope."

He had a sneaking suspicion he knew what it contained and hoped against hope he was wrong. Unfortunately, he confirmed his guess the instant he read the work order Cord had called about. "What if I don't want this gift?" he asked tightly.

"Then you can have the other one. It's sort of an either/or proposition. You can have whichever one you want, but not both."

He cautiously removed the gift wrapping on the second gift, surprised to discover that it really was a sketchpad. He flipped open the cover. To his delight he realized she'd drawn a mockup for a new storybook, the futuristic adventures of a mischievous preschooler who bore a striking resemblance to Noelle, and a broken-down robot the image of Emo, whose function was to read and respond to human emotion. But because he got everything wrong, he'd been sent to the junkyard, where the little girl found him and carted him home.

The storyline was adorable, funny and poignant, and he savored each and every page. Toward the end of the story, the two were discovered by the authorities and the robot had to either get his emotion reader to work or the little girl would be forced to return him to the scrap heap.

The final test came in front of a stern-faced tribunal. "What do I feel?" the little girl asked her robot, her heart in her eyes.

Justice gently flipped the page. But instead of a conclusion he found himself staring at a blank sheet of paper. He looked at Daisy in bewilderment. "I don't understand. There's no ending."

"That's because I can't end it…until you tell me how. If you can't, you'll have to accept the work order. Either/or, Justice."

He closed his eyes. He knew how this story concluded. He'd known all along. Until today, he hadn't believed himself capable of the emotion. But not anymore. Not when everything he wanted was on the line…a line he'd drawn and dared Daisy to step over. She hadn't stepped over it, she'd leaped over it, kicking his line into nonexistence.

He closed the sketch pad and picked up his gift to her, setting it down in front of her. It didn't take much imagination to guess what he'd so awkwardly wrapped. Without a word she stripped away the wrapping paper to reveal Emo.

"Turn it on," he encouraged.

She pressed the appropriate button on the robot's control panel helmet. Emo hummed to life. "Hello, Emo," she said.

The head turned in circles, the bright aquamarine eyes scanning the room, scanning the people one by one. "I love you. I'm hungry. Would you like a nice cup of tea?"

Jett burst out laughing and Noelle clapped her hands, babbling in excitement. "Emo," Justice said. "How do I feel?"

"You would like a nice cup of tea," Emo chirped.

It was all Justice could do to keep from yanking his hair out by the roots. "Damn it, you good for nothing bucket of bolts! You were supposed to tell Daisy I love her!"

For a split second no one moved. No one even drew breath. Then Daisy flew into his arms. "I believe you just did tell me. And to be honest, I'd much rather hear it from you than from Emo." She gazed up at him, her own love spilling out like rays of sunshine on a cloudless day. "And that was exactly the line I hoped to use to end the story I wrote."

Justice blew out a sigh. "I'm sorry, Daisy. I worked all night on him. I thought…" He trailed off, shaking his head.

"That he could tell me what you couldn't?"

"No!" He took a deep breath. "No. I do love you, Daisy. I

love you with all my heart. But I didn't think you'd believe me, not after I resisted saying the words for so long."

"You figured if Emo said them for you, if he read your emotions, I'd believe you?"

"Yes." He dropped his forehead to hers. "I've spent twenty-seven years, two months and twenty-six days believing I couldn't feel. It was easier to believe. Less painful."

She gave him a tremulous smile. "And now?"

"Now it's more painful not to say the words," he admitted. "I can't bear the thought of losing you and the rest of our family. Please don't let the story end with a blank page. Please be the one who'll give me a real family, not an apprentice family. Who'll always be there for me if I'm ever hurt again. Take a chance. Marry me, Daisy."

Her smile grew, blinding him with its brilliance. "I'll marry you, on two conditions."

Aw, hell. "Which are?"

"First, Joint Condition Two. I'm allowed downstairs whenever I want."

His tawny gaze grew brighter than the Christmas tree lights. "I'll agree to that if you'll agree to Joint Condition Three," he bargained.

"Which is?"

"You create a room upstairs just for the two of us. One on the south side of the house."

"But…" Uncertainty filled her expression. "That's the sunny side."

"So it is." Warmth filled his eyes. "It's time to leave the darkness behind and step out into the sunlight, don't you think?" He pulled her closer. "Now will you marry me?"

She nodded, hope springing to life and filling her expression with joy. "If you can answer just one more tiny question."

"And what question is that?"

"How do you feel, Justice?" she whispered.

He could hear the collective inhale as everyone waited for his response. When he spoke, he spoke from the heart. "I feel…happy. Like our story is just beginning."

"Oh, Justice." Tears of delight filled her eyes. "And what a story it will be."

"One for the books," he agreed and feathered a kiss across her mouth. "After all, you taught a robot to feel."

"No, Justice." She returned his kiss, their first real kiss. "I taught a man to love."

* * * * *

*Jett and Pretorious haven't quite given
up the Perfect program yet.
Don't miss out on
MORE THAN PERFECT
Spring 2012!*

PASSION

For a spicier, decidedly hotter read—
this is your destination for romance!

COMING NEXT MONTH
AVAILABLE DECEMBER 6, 2011

#2125 THE TEMPORARY MRS. KING
Kings of California
Maureen Child

#2126 IN BED WITH THE OPPOSITION
Texas Cattleman's Club: The Showdown
Kathie DeNosky

#2127 THE COWBOY'S PRIDE
Billionaires and Babies
Charlene Sands

#2128 LESSONS IN SEDUCTION
Sandra Hyatt

#2129 AN INNOCENT IN PARADISE
Kate Carlisle

#2130 A MAN OF HIS WORD
Sarah M. Anderson

HDCNM1111

REQUEST YOUR FREE BOOKS!
2 FREE NOVELS PLUS 2 FREE GIFTS!

❧ Harlequin® *Desire*

ALWAYS POWERFUL, PASSIONATE AND PROVOCATIVE

*Lucy Flemming and Ross Mitchell shared a magical,
sexy Christmas weekend together six years ago.
This Christmas, history may repeat itself when they find
themselves stranded in a major snowstorm...
and alone at last.*

Read on for a sneak peek from
IT HAPPENED ONE CHRISTMAS
by Leslie Kelly.

Available December 2011, only from Harlequin® Blaze™.

EYEING THE GRAY, THICK SKY through the expansive wall of windows, Lucy began to pack up her photography gear. The Christmas party was winding down, only a dozen or so people remaining on this floor, which had been transformed from cubicles and meeting rooms to a holiday funland. She smiled at those nearest to her, then, seeing the glances at her silly elf hat, she reached up to tug it off her head.

Before she could do it, however, she heard a voice. A deep, male voice—smooth and sexy, and so not Santa's.

"I appreciate you filling in on such short notice. I've heard you do a terrific job."

Lucy didn't turn around, letting her brain process what she was hearing. Her whole body had stiffened, the hairs on the back of her neck standing up, her skin tightening into tiny goose bumps. Because that voice sounded so familiar. *Impossibly* familiar.

It can't be.

"It sounds like the kids had a great time."

Unable to stop herself, Lucy began to turn around, wondering if her ears—and all her other senses—were deceiving her. After all, six years was a long time, the mind could play tricks. What were the odds that she'd bump into *him*, here? And today of all days. December 23.

Six years exactly. Was that really possible?

One look—and the accompanying frantic thudding of her heart—and she knew her ears and brain were working just fine. Because it was *him*.

"Oh, my God," he whispered, shocked, frozen, staring as thoroughly as she was. "Lucy?"

She nodded slowly, not taking her eyes off him, wondering why the years had made him even more attractive than ever. It didn't seem fair. Not when she'd spent the past six years thinking he must have started losing that thick, golden-brown hair, or added a spare tire to that trim, muscular form.

No.

The man was gorgeous. Truly, without-a-doubt, mouth-wateringly handsome, every bit as hot as he'd been the first time she'd laid eyes on him. She'd been twenty-two, he one year older.

They'd shared an amazing holiday season.

And had never seen one another again.

Until now.

Find out what happens in
IT HAPPENED ONE CHRISTMAS
by Leslie Kelly.
Available December 2011, only from Harlequin® Blaze™

ROMANTIC
SUSPENSE

USA TODAY BESTSELLING AUTHOR

MARIE FERRARELLA

Brings you another exciting installment from

CAVANAUGH
JUSTICE

A Cavanaugh Christmas

When Detective Kaitlyn Two Feathers follows a kidnapping case outside her jurisdiction, she enlists the aid of Detective Thomas Cavelli. Still reeling from the discovery that his father was a Cavanaugh, Thomas takes the case, thinking it will be a nice distraction…until Kaitlyn becomes his ultimate distraction. As the case heats up and time is running out, Thomas must prove to Kaitlyn that he is trustworthy and risk it all for the one thing they both never thought they'd find—love.

Available November 22 wherever books are sold!

LAURA MARIE ALTOM
brings you
another touching tale from

When family tragedy forces Wyatt Buckhorn to pair up
with his longtime secret crush, Natalie Poole, and care
for the Buckhorn clan's seven children, Wyatt worries
he's in over his head. Fearing his shameful secret will
be exposed, Wyatt tries to fight his growing attraction
to Natalie. As Natalie begins to open up to Wyatt,
he starts yearning for a family of his own—a family
with Natalie. But can Wyatt trust his heart enough
to reveal his secret?

A Baby in His Stocking

Available December
wherever books are sold!